GUARDIANS
of GA'HOOLE

THE RISE OF
A LEGEND

GUARDIANS
of GA'HOOLE

THE RISE OF
A LEGEND

KATHRYN LASKY

SCHOLASTIC PRESS / NEW YORK

Library of Congress Cataloging-in-Publication Data

Lasky, Kathryn.
The rise of a legend / Kathryn Lasky. — 1st ed.
p. cm. — (Guardians of Ga'hoole)
Summary: In this prequel, Ezylryb the Screech owl recounts the story of
his life in the Northern Kingdoms — his rise through the ranks of the
Kielian Army, his brother's betrayal, and his friendship with Octavia
the snake, to finally become a Guardian of Ga'Hoole.
ISBN 978-0-545-50978-7 (jacketed hardcover) —
1. Owls — Juvenile fiction. [1. Owls — Fiction.] I. Title. II.
Series: Lasky, Kathryn. Guardians of Ga'Hoole.
PZ7.L3274Rh 2013
813.54 — dc23
2013006691

10 9 8 7 6 5 4 3 2   13 14 15 16 17

Printed in the U.S.A.   23

First edition, August 2013

Book design by Whitney Lyle

For Evan Weaver, who inspired this book.

— K. L.

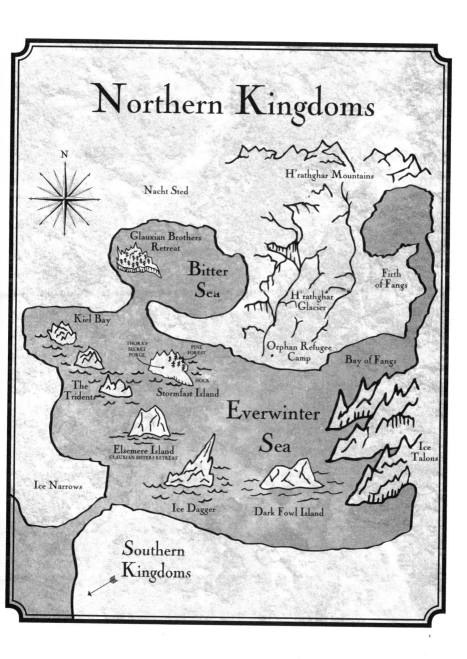

Northern Kingdoms

N

H'rathghar Mountains

Nacht Sted

Glauxian Brothers
Retreat

Bitter
Sea

Firth
of Fangs

H'rathghar
Glacier

Kiel Bay

Orphan Refugee
Camp

Bay of Fangs

THORA'S
SECRET
FORGE

PINE
FOREST

HOCK

The
Tridents

Stormfast Island

Everwinter
Sea

Ice
Talons

Elsemere Island
GLAUXIAN SISTERS RETREAT

Ice Narrows

Ice Dagger

Dark Fowl Island

Southern
Kingdoms

Prologue

Tonight something odd happened. A young Barn Owl and three of his companions showed up here. Blown right out of a force-eight gale. A raging thing it was, that gale, full of slop and ice. Couldn't see for racdrops out there. These four had been traveling together for some time. They call themselves the Band, or a Band, as if they're special or something. Perhaps they are. It's the Barn Owl, the one called Soren, who interests me. There's something about him that took me back to my own youth. It stirred me deeply.

So I decided to put aside this book I've been working on, the third volume in *Weather Systems and Their Structure: How to Fly Them, Analyze Them, and Survive Them*, and turn instead to something a little less academic, a little less dry. Indeed, a story drenched with blood from endless wars and also tears, both happy and sad, of love, betrayal, and of hope.

The Barn Owl's just a lad and does not know what he's in for. I certainly didn't. Oh my, I was such an innocent — if one can call an aspiring warrior "innocent." And what am I now but a reclusive scholar, a scientist in a world still boiling with violence. I have chosen a different path. However, once I was a very different owl. So different.

Now I begin my own story. I shall call it simply *The Book of Ezylryb.*

THE BOOK OF

EZYLRYB

THE OWLET
MOONS

CHAPTER 1

I Hatch Out

The first crack in the egg that held me occurred just before midnight. My mum and da weren't there, of course, as the action in the century-long War of the Ice Claws had heated up and they were both away fighting. So they'd gotten a hire broody for the egg — common practice in the war-torn Northern Kingdoms. When my first crack started, the hire broody, Gundesfyrr, sent out Mrs. Grinkle, our nest-maid snake, to inform the neighbors. Hatchings were treasured occasions, particularly during times of war, for every new chick was viewed as a potential fighter. Most likely, everyone bent over my shell urging me to soldier on in my first battle — getting out of this egg that had sheltered me for nearly two moons.

"C'mon, chickie! Follow in the flight marks of your da — the old general!"

"And his mum, don't forget his mum! The commando." The words were muffled through the shell and I really didn't understand much. But I would soon learn that my mum was a commando in the Ice Dagger unit, and Da was supreme commander of all the allied forces of the Kielian League, which included the famous Frost Beaks as well as the Hot Blades and other divisions. In short, they didn't come home too much.

Don't feel sorry for me. This was the way it was back in those days on Stormfast Island in the western part of the Everwinter Sea. It would have been mighty queer for an owlet to have both parents around. Almost embarrassing, quite frankly.

I soldiered on in the shell, knocking my brains out trying to get out of there, although most of the work was done with my egg tooth. *Peck, peck, ram.* Then pry a bit, rest, then peck some more. Soon I had opened another crack. There was a great hooray and then a gasp. Someone had just arrived.

"What's she doing here?" a voice said in stunned disbelief.

It was, I am told, my tantya Hanja. The good cheer and boisterous spirits receded immediately. Tantya Hanja was Mum's sister. The two of them were as different as sisters could be. Tantya Hanja wasn't a military type. Glaux, no! She would have been disastrous in battle. Instead, she was a quiet little thing, whose whiskers seemed longer than her wings. She had a funny style of flying, a permanent list to port, which disqualified her for military service. To compensate, her starboard wing had grown much larger than the other, and she seemed a bit lopsided. But she got around.

Everyone called her Prinka Hanja. "Prinka" meant "poor" in Krakish, the language of the Northern Kingdoms. They felt sorry for her because she couldn't hunt as well as others. Therefore, she led an itinerant life, visiting relatives. Our family dreaded it when she showed up. She had a knack for appearing when something bad was going to happen. So when she arrived the very night I was hatching out, my broody, Gundesfyrr, began to tremble fiercely and crouch over my egg protectively.

"Oh, good Glaux!" Gundesfyrr nearly keeled over as Tantya Hanja approached the nest with me in it.

"Would love to have a peek. I had a haggish time getting here," Tantya Hanja said. "The winds were against me the whole way. I see I have arrived just in time. First crack already!"

"Second crack, actually," Gundesfyrr said weakly.

"Can I tidy up here a bit in preparation for the new chick? Would you like me to gather some moss? It's always comfy, isn't it, for the little ones as they're almost bald after they hatch out. And here, Gundesfyrr, let me give you some down." Hanja poked her beak into the thick feathers of her primaries and plucked out the downy ones beneath.

"Oh, that really isn't necessary!" Gundesfyrr shrieked.

"Don't screech, dearie! Not just after second crack. That

could jiggle things up the wrong way for the exit crack. Now we wouldn't want that, would we?"

Gundesfyrr exchanged a horrified glance with Elfstrom, a neighboring Snowy, who had entered the hollow and clamped his beak shut at the sight of Hanja. Elfstrom had seen more battles in his lifetime than my two parents put together. He was on leave from a striker unit after a fierce battle in the Ice Narrows. Very little unnerved this veteran commander, but the sight of Tantya Hanja did.

"There you go," Tantya Hanja said, tucking some of her down into the brooding nest. "Now I'll be back in two shakes of my tail feathers with some moss for the little one. Bet he'll be handsome like his big brother, Edvard. Such a handsome Screech, that one." Just as she was about to leave, she turned and said, "Nearly forgot. Might as well take some of my whiskers. They grow so long this time of year that my talons get tangled in them."

Gundesfyrr didn't need to worry. There were no odd jiggles to interfere with the exit crack. I hatched out just fine.

Of course, my eyes were still sealed shut. I could see nothing but I could hear voices muttering about Tantya Hanja. I couldn't make that much sense out of it. It just came to me in fragments.

"Why did *she* have to show up?"

"Always an ill omen."

"But look, he's just fine."

Who was "she"? Who was "hesjustfine"? Was that a very long name? And then suddenly, the words stopped and there were terrible sobbing sounds. No words, just long, agonized cries interrupted by short, wet blubberings and gasps. Someone called, "Edvard is dead!" What was an "Edvard"? What was "dead"? I would very soon learn that Edvard had been my brother, and a messenger had arrived from the Hot Blades unit, saying that he had been killed in action over the Firth of Fangs.

So as I entered the world, more or less staggering from my shell, I was surrounded by crying adults, Gundesfyrr, Elfstrom the Snowy, a neighboring Barred Owl couple from across the way, as well as three or four Kielian nest-maid snakes.[1]

"Oh, dear," sobbed Mrs. Grinkle, a very elderly nest-maid snake. "I guess you're the man of the nest now!" she said, looking at me — me, who still had the goo of egg yolk on my unsightly featherless body. Everybody began sobbing anew. I had no idea what she was talking about. I started pecking at the slime left in the fractured cup of the egg. This is an owlet's first meal and as such provides the occasion for a First

---

1 Although this is not an academic book, old ways die hard and I am compelled here and there to add a talonmark. So let me make it quite clear right now that Kielian snakes are not blind like Hoolian nest-maid snakes. Nor are their scales the pinkish-coral color of the Hoolian snakes, but are greenish-blue, which ranges from turquoise to azure and cobalt. These snakes also have a heavier build and are quite muscular.

Ceremony. First Slime it's called. But in the tumultuous grief of the moment, everyone seemed to have forgotten this except for Tantya Hanja, who had returned with soft moss for the nest. Calmly, she began singing:

> *Lick the slime,*
> *There is time.*
> *Dear owlet,*
> *You have hatched.*
> *Now you feed*
> *As is decreed.*
> *May you grow big and strong,*
> *Fledge your wings,*
> *Learn to sing.*
> *But this is your first feed,*
> *So to you we say, Glauxspeed!*

Hanja continued, "Now we must all pull ourselves together because I think this is a precious little chick here. I have a feeling he's bound for greatness."

"Oh, dear," Mrs. Grinkle the nest-maid snake whispered. "What she feels is greatness is sometimes tragedy — the tragedy of heroism like dear Edvard!"

Two days later, Tantya Hanja left and there was a great sigh of relief at our end of Stormfast Island. And before I knew it, it was time for my First Insect ceremony. But even more memorable would be my First Meat ceremony, for my mum and da had returned by then.

CHAPTER 2

Fuzzball to Fledgling

The owlet years can be divided into three stages. The first is commonly called the Fuzzball stage, and the subsequent ones are the Fledgling and the Flight stages. They are often referred to as the Three Fs. The Fuzzball period is named after an owlet's lack of true feathers. Instead, we are covered in unsightly patches of downy fluff. All adult owls think we are extremely cute, absolutely adorable. How quickly they forget! If you are an owl chick, you're embarrassed about being half naked, and because you are half naked, you're always cold and dependent on mature owls to cuddle and comfort you to keep you warm. Worst of all, you can't fly! You examine yourself every five seconds for any trace of budging points, those tiny little knobs of flesh where feathers begin to poke through.

In the Fledgling stage, a chick begins to learn how to branch, which will ultimately lead to flying. Of course, in the Northern Kingdoms, there aren't many trees, so branching per se is difficult. Instead, we have to use rocky, often ice-sheathed outcroppings. My family was lucky, for we lived in one of the few stands of trees on Stormfast Island. The hollow in which I hatched was in a slender pine.

But I digress. It was long before I branched that I had my First Meat ceremony, and this was when I met my parents for the first time.

"They're coming! They're coming!" Gundesfyrr hooted.

"Who's coming?" I chirped.

"Your mum, your da, back from the last battle near the Ice Talons, and just in time for your First Meat ceremony."

"I get to eat meat!" I did a little jump. Meat was actually more exciting to me than my mum and da. Remember, I had never really seen a mum or a da. But I'd seen a lot of meat. Gundesfyrr and her friends were always chomping on rockmunks, a kind of chipmunk that lived in the rocky cliffs on Stormfast, or lemmings or voles. Sometimes they even ate fish. The Fish Owls dove for them off one point of the island. But all I ever got to eat during my Fuzzball stage, beyond the slime from my eggshell, were carefully selected insects. Insects don't have meat and, most significantly, they don't have blood. The scent of blood when Gundesfyrr and her friends came in with freshly slaughtered rodents was enough to drive me *yoickers!*[2] So I was beside myself when I heard that my parents were coming and bringing me a plump vole!

---

2   Many Krakish words are similar to Hoolian ones. "Yoickers" is the word for "crazy" in Krakish. In Hoolian language, it is simply "yoicks."

The only problem was that when Mum and Da flew into the hollow, I nearly yarped. It wasn't the vole with its steaming guts slithering out from the slash of my mum's talons that made me want to yarp. It was Mum who gave me a fright. She only had one eye! Where the other eye should have been was a pit leaking blood through a seam that had been coarsely stitched across it.

Do all mums just have one eye? I wondered. I couldn't help myself, and I shrieked when she bent over me. Suddenly, I knew — this was the face of war!

"Oh dear, my patch must have slipped off," my mum said. She quickly reached up with her port talon and pulled down a small piece of lemming fur to cover the eye pit. "I didn't mean to scare you, Lyze. No, never! You are a dear little thing."

Gundesfyrr nudged me a bit, then whispered, "Greet your mum, dear."

"Oh, let him get used to me. I know it must be hard. I'm just glad I've got one eye left to see him with."

"Hello, Mum. Sorry, I — I —" I was trembling. I just couldn't look at her.

"Never mind, dear. You'll get used to it." But would I? And what if I didn't? Everyone was a warrior, a soldier. All anyone ever talked about was war. This was our life, why owlets often knew their hire broody and nest-maid snakes better than their own mums and das. I knew I would have to toughen up, so I dared myself to look at the horrible gash that ran out from under the lemming fur, like a jagged thunderbolt down her face. Did I doubt war at this point? I'm not sure. After all, I was just an owlet. But I might have doubted myself and whether I could be an honorable member of the Kielian League.

Rask was my father's name. It was an old-soldier name and meant fast or quick. But he was not quick enough, apparently. One side of his face had been seared and he was missing his whiskers! Not a pretty sight. But not nearly as shocking somehow as my mum's missing eye.

"What a tough little owl we got here! A veritable *whiskerspritz!*" my father said. "*Whiskerspritz*" was a term of endearment for a young Whiskered Screech Owl. It meant "full of spirit." I felt anything but, and truthfully I felt a bit cheated. My parents were legends on Stormfast, but heroes or not, one was missing an eye, and the other, half his whiskers. And then I realized that it was shameful for the son of heroes to be thinking this way.

"Don't let this bother you, son." My da tapped the whiskerless side of his face.

"Do you think they'll grow back?" I asked.

"Probably no more chance than your mum here has of growing another eye. But we showed them, didn't we, Ulfa?" He turned and nuzzled my mum.

"Where was the battle, sir?" Gundesfyrr asked quietly. Nay,

not just quietly, but reverently. She looked straight into their mangled faces as if paying homage to their scars. *I must try and do the same*, I thought.

"First Ice Talon between there and the Ice Narrows. Just a skirmish, really. They got her eye and my whiskers, but we got them! By Glaux, we got 'em! We were the only ones in our units who were injured. Very lucky we were. Very lucky."

Lucky? I thought. *They call this luck?* All I could think about was my mum's eye — somewhere at the bottom of the Everwinter Sea. However, when they started to speak of the strategy and the weapons, I must admit it interested me. War seemed like a strange but violent puzzle to me.

"We left our mark, didn't we, Sweet Gizz?" My da nuzzled my mum's chest feathers.

"Darned hootin'! Your da raked off half a Great Horned's beak, and I snapped off not one, but two, of the other fellow's talons."

"Mercy!" exclaimed Gundesfyrr. "And you having just lost your eye!"

"I know. Not sure how I did it. It's one of those instances in battle when you don't think, you just do. Something rushed through me like a hurricane-force wind and just . . . just propelled me. I didn't feel any pain, any anger even, just a passion to destroy."

"It's called being a soldier," my da said. "You'll do it, too, someday. Someday, young'un!" He turned to me almost jubilantly, as if anticipating the courage I wasn't sure I'd have.

I wondered if I would ever be a soldier, a true soldier.

"When can I have my meat? I'm hungry," I said.

"That's the spirit, lad!" my father boomed.

"Yes, let's get on with the First Meat ceremony!" My mum's voice rang out joyfully.

Before I knew it, the hollow was crowded. For this ceremony, my mother stripped the fur from the vole, and then my father stripped the meat from the bone. It is more digestible this way for a young chick. We are not expected to swallow the creature whole, like the grown-ups do. Our gizzards aren't up to it.

Mum and Da were around for a good while, as they had been granted a long leave. And before I knew it, I had passed through my First-Fur-on-Meat ceremony, which meant I got to eat the entire vole skin off the bone but with the fur. The fur tickled when it went down. And finally, it was time for my First-Meat-on-Bones ceremony. For that, they always bring back quite a small rodent, either a baby or one of the dwarf rats that scramble about on the beaches of Stormfast. There's a bit of a knack to eating a creature whole.

"No, dear, headfirst. They slide down the gullet easier that way," my mother counseled. Once I got the creature oriented right (I believe it was a dwarf rat), I took it down with one gulp followed by a very loud belch.

"You sound like your old man, lad." My da laughed, 'and gave a loud belch himself.

"Honestly, Rask!" Mum sighed.

And then, of course, it was time to sing the belching song that celebrates the first time an owlet eats his first whole animal with meat, fur, and bones. The song is called "The Uuul-glutch," a word that looks almost unpronounceable here on the page and resembles the sound of a deep belch that can only be made by animals with gizzards. Owls essentially have two stomachs. The first is a stomach like that most animals have. The second is the gizzard, a thick-walled and very muscular stomach made for grinding up grit and packing in small bones and fur. *Uuul-glutch* is the sound made when something passes from the first stomach to the second one, the gizzard.

Gundesfyrr started the singing:

Uuul-glutch! Uuul-glutch!
Let the sound ring out.
There's a little critter that
No longer scampers about.
Lodged in the gizzard

Fast and cozy it does lay.
And soon a pellet is on its way.

And very soon it was. Mum and Da led me to the edge of the hollow and I yarped my first real pellet. I was growing up fast!

CHAPTER 3

First Feathers

It was a fine pellet. "Exquisite," Mum said. "Manly," said my father. Then they had a nice little spat, where Mum said that there was no such thing as a manly pellet any more than there could be a feminine or girlish pellet. But to me, the most thrilling thing of all was standing on the rim of the hollow and looking outside for the first time. I felt the cold air, the flurry of snow in my face; I saw the slender limbs of the pine tree in which we lived and the beautiful green needles poking through the snow-laden branches. And in a neighboring tree, I saw an owlet teetering on a branch.

"What's he doing, Da?"

"Learning to branch."

"I want to do that!"

"You will, you will."

"No! I mean now. Right now!"

"You haven't fledged yet, silly," my mother said. "You have to have at least a few feathers before you can branch. Now, come inside. You're shivering."

"No, I'm not!"

"You're cold, dear," Gundesfyrr said.

"I am NOT cold!" I said. But in truth, the skin between my ugly patches had turned almost blue. What a beauty I was!

From that moment, I was on high alert for any signs of budging. Every day, when my parents weren't looking, I would creep to the edge of the hollow and watch the owlet across the way. His name was Moss, and I was insanely jealous. He was a Snowy and had hatched out the very same night I had. Perhaps he beat me out of the shell by an hour or two, but no more. I would say he was a big owlet, but he was not unusually large for a Snowy. It was just that Snowies are naturally much larger birds than Whiskered Screeches. And that hour or so seemed to have given him a feather up. Yes, he was fledging out fast.

When I asked why Moss had fledged so quickly, all the grown-ups around me replied, "Well, Snowies just do that." It was one of those irritating answers that adults give and expect young'uns to take on faith. Well, not me. I take very few things on faith. Not then. Not now.

To my grim little eyes, Moss, swathed in these gorgeous fluffy white feathers with several dark splotches, seemed huge. And he was branching beautifully. Budging, branching, flying — these were all called "flight marks" in an owlet's progress toward wing mastery.

I knew it was only a matter of a few nights until Moss would be actually flying. FLYING! And I would be stuck in this ferschtucken hollow. Unfortunately, I had the stupidity to blurt out the word "ferschtucken" one evening when I was complaining about not being a fledgling, and I earned myself a firm swat on my tail fluff from Mum. "Ferschtucken" is a curse word. I didn't know this at the time, but when I stood on the rim of the hollow and observed the world outside, I heard a lot of things from warriors on leave, a lot of swearwords. I had even heard my father say "ferschtucken" when he was talking with an old Kielian League buddy about the action on the front.

Then there was a terrifying story I heard one evening when my parents thought I was sound asleep. They spoke in low, hushed voices, and maybe it was the very softness of their voices that alerted me.

"Did you hear?" my mum asked.

"Hear what, Ulfa?" Da's voice was tense.

"The news from over in the Bay of Fangs — a Snowy family." My mum did not wait for Da to answer. It was as if she had to get her story out. "They say it was in a pine grove, maybe just like ours. Quiet, you know." Her voice dropped lower, and I had to strain to hear. "He comes up with two of his lieutenants. And there were these Snowies —" She seemed to gulp. "Well, their young'un had just hatched out, maybe the night before, and he was trying to recruit them for the Ice Talons League. I guess they refused and he went mad, yoickers, completely berserk, then seized the young'un. Stuffed him in a botkin and screamed, 'I'll make a soldier out of your babe if not you!' He killed the parents in front of the owlet's very eyes. He did that, Rask, and it isn't just a rumor. It's the truth!"

I felt my own gizzard freeze when I heard this. *"He!"* I knew already who *he* was: Bylyric, the commander of the Ice Talons League. They said he was not simply ruthless, but completely mad. There were many names for him — the Tyrant of the Ice Talons, and then the Orphan Maker. I wrapped my wings around myself and tried to go to sleep.

I wanted to be a soldier like my mum and da, but their conversation had shaken me. Bylyric was evil. Every owlet knew that from the time he or she hatched out. Bylyric was the reason that the war was fought. But Bylyric was not that old. He had not always been around, and it seemed as if my parents could barely remember why the war had begun more than one hundred years ago. If Bylyric was killed, would the war keep going? Had something been set in motion a long, long time ago and no one knew how to stop it? But before I could draw any conclusions, I suddenly had an itchy feeling in my starboard wing. I ran my tongue — yes, owls do have tongues — over the itch and, by Glaux, there was a tiny bump. *It can't be!*

I thought. *It can't be!* But it was. "I'm budging! I'm budging!" I screeched.

Mum came running over. "Really!" she exclaimed with delight. "Let me see, Lyzie."

"Don't call me 'Lyzie.' I am about to fledge! When can I go to Dark Fowl? When? When? When?"

The flight to Dark Fowl Island marked the end of the owlet moons. It was when an owl proved his or her wings and could start to train to become a cadet. This island to the southeast of Stormfast in the Everwinter Sea was practically all one ever heard about on Stormfast for many reasons. First, Dark Fowl Island was where some of the best weapons in all of the Northern Kingdoms were forged. Orf the Rogue smith presided over the forge that had come down to him through his fore-bears, a long line of Great Grays with an uncanny ability to understand not just metal, but ice as well. He was as much a hero as any soldier.

It was just going to kill me if Moss got to go to Dark Fowl before I did. By this time, Moss had fledged out gorgeously and was now doing an admirable job of branching — branching and bragging! Every time I looked out from the hollow, he was carrying on about how by the next dwenking of the moon, when it was as thin as the finest filament of down, he would be winging his way to Dark Fowl. I couldn't stand to watch his progress, and yet I could not tear myself away.

I hopped over to the Hollow's entrance just in time to see Moss's father toss a dead vole to the ground. Moss went into a plunge, called a kill spiral. It was a game known as "lob and gob." Owlets who had just learned to branch played it all the time, as it was the best preparation for hunting. As soon as a fledging owlet learned to fly, he or she would hunt for food. I had only played lob and gob in the hollow with Mum or Da, or sometimes our new nest-maid snake, Gilda. They would fling about a dead mouse and I would try to loft myself into the dim hollow air, get as far as I could, and then pounce on it. Talon placement is very important. One needs to grasp the creature immediately, secure "talon lock," and then puncture its lungs or heart.

"Watch this!" Moss hooted across from the tree where he lived. "This is going to be great, Da." But it really wasn't his father he was addressing, for he always looked my way. Then he would do something rather spectacular for a branching owl, and his father would flap his own huge white wings in approval. Moss's wings were not pure white. Not yet. Immature Snowies have a dappling of black feathers mixed in with the white ones. They are actually quite striking, especially in comparison to a Screech like myself.

When I finally fledged completely, I would be of a rather drab plumage — grayish-brownish. "Ish" — that's me, not quite one thing or another. One might even say we Whiskered

Screech Owls are rather dingy looking. The one feature that redeems us from this drabness is, ironically, our call. I say "ironically" because, after all, we are named Screech Owls, but our calls can be the most mellifluous sounds you have ever heard. Some say our voices are like starlight or like the sound of the stars singing. Some have compared the lower register of our hoots to the sound of a wooden flute, like those found in the ruins of the Others' castles and palaces. Our calls are nothing like the harsh gruff barkings of a Snowy Owl, of which I had been hearing quite enough, thank you very much.

But at last came the fateful night that was to mark the beginning of a most unlikely friendship. It was the night that Moss flew for the first time and I took my first tiny little jump from the branch just outside the hollow to another that was no distance at all away.

To me, this little jump was a triumph. But the hoots that clawed the air to herald a great feat were not for me, but for Moss! Moss had completed his first circumnavigation of Hock Point at the far end of the island. I was furious that Moss's flight eclipsed my little jump. To fly to the Hock, rest, and then come back was one thing, but to fly around the tip of the point and all the way back was extraordinary for an owlet. Moss might as well have flown to the moon. "Can't be long now, son! Next stop, Dark Fowl!" his father boomed.

"Ever see anything like it?" An uncle came up and thwacked

Moss with his port wing. I blinked. If anyone had thwacked me like that, I would have fallen off my branch. My mother alighted on the branch next to me.

"You did an admirable job, Lyze. Very graceful." I shrank down at her words. She was so obviously trying to boost my spirits in the shadow of Moss's spectacular achievement.

"What are you wilfing about, dear? You just branched, for Glaux's sake!" She nodded her head vigorously as if to drive this idea home. Her bandanna slipped a bit, exposing the eyeless, crinkled pit.

"Mum," I whispered. "Your bandanna." She flicked me a rather harsh look from her good eye and adjusted the bandanna. I felt terrible for even mentioning it.

Meanwhile in the next tree over, Moss was absolutely wallowing in the accolades his relatives were showering upon him. There was much talk about how it was such a shame his mum could not be there to witness his great achievement. Repeatedly, he lifted off from a branch to demonstrate how, when she finally arrived, he would show her a certain maneuver he had made when kitibit winds were swirling about the tip of the Hock.[3] The kitibits often picked up bits of debris, seaweed, and

---

3   The kitibit winds, not to be confused with the much more fearsome katabatic winds, are minor swirls that kick up around peninsulas and points of land, creating wind holes or vortexes. They require a certain amount of skill to fly around them and avoid the suction dimples.

even the odd, tiny flying fish or minnow. Moss was now brandishing a small bunch of sea grapes that had a dead minnow entwined in them.

"Would you look at this!" he exclaimed. "And a minnow!"

"Eat it! Eat it!" his older sister cried out in an awful grating hoot. "It's good luck."

"Old wives' tales," someone barked.

"Old wives! Speaking of old wives!" It was Moss's father, his beak dropping. "Glaux, is it really? Hrenna! My dear Hrenna!"

Just then a Snowy landed, shouting, "Moss! Moss! My dear son!"

All I remember from that moment is that Moss suddenly seemed to wilt. All the bluster went out of him, and oddly enough, he cast a glance toward me, a sly, almost frightened glance. Moss and his immediate family disappeared into the hollow, but outside the celebration continued. It would be a few nights until I saw Moss again.

CHAPTER 4

Moss and Me

My father suggested that we accept the invitation to visit Moss's hollow since his mum had returned now. All returning warriors liked to exchange news from the front. Mum asked me if I wanted to join them.

"Is Moss going to be there?" I asked. I really didn't relish watching him brag about all his accomplishments.

"Well, yes, of course, dear."

"Isn't it high time he flew off to Dark Fowl? I mean, he did all the steps. Proved himself," I said rather dismissively, perhaps without gravitas, the dignity required when speaking of such things. My mother cocked her head and made no attempt to adjust the bandanna that had slipped with this sudden motion.

"Lyze, I'm not sure what your problem is here. But I don't like your attitude. We're invited over, and you are coming. Fledgling jealousy is an unbecoming trait." She paused. "Some say it can even make your barbules grow crisscross." That, I was sure, was an old wives' tale. On every flight feather there are tiny, nearly invisible hooks called barbules that interlock to produce an even surface over which wind can glide. A favorite scolding for young owlets was "Don't do that or your barbules will come out 'whiffy skew.'"

Mum squared her shoulders and gave me a harsh glare with her one eye. "You shall be coming with us. You shall congratulate Moss on his magnificent flight, and you shall behave yourself in a manner that becomes the son of the supreme commander of all the allied forces of the Kielian League, and the commando of the Ice Dagger unit. Is this understood?"

I lifted my starboard talon and gave what I hoped was a crisp salute even though I was shaking terribly. Neither my mother nor my father had ever spoken to me this way. I felt a terrible crinkle in my gizzard, and I tried to avoid my mother's gaze, but she thrust herself toward me and shoved her face so close to mine that her feathers swept my cheek. She cocked her head so that terrible, scarred pit where her eye had been filled my vision. It loomed like a burnt crater.

"Take a good look, my dear. You want a perfect mother, do you? One that is not scarred. You know what did that?" I remained silent. She took a deep breath. "You know what took my eye?"

"No, Mum."

"An ice splinter. And an inferior one at that. I flew right into it. Never saw it coming. Had I not been flying at fever speed, the damage wouldn't have been so bad. But it was, and now you have a flawed, imperfect mother."

"Flawed in body," my father added. "But not in spirit. Not in valor."

"Is . . . is being a soldier . . . the . . . the only . . . uh . . . way one can fight?" I asked. My parents blinked at me. Their large yellow eyes seemed to dull with incomprehension. I might as well have been speaking a foreign language.

"What in the name of Glaux are you talking about, son?" Da asked.

"Uh . . . uh . . . nothing. Forget it."

"Yes." Mum nodded emphatically. "Forget it!"

I looked down at a bark worm that was creeping across the hollow floor. I felt lower than that creeping, spineless, soft-bodied piece of squish that the nest-maid snakes feasted on.

My mother spotted it as well. "Where is that new nest-maid snake? What's her name?"

"Gilda?" I ventured.

"Yes, that's the one. She's not as good as Mrs. Grinkle. I can't wait until Mrs. Grinkle gets back from visiting her relatives. Gilda!" she called out.

"Yes, ma'am, yes!" Gilda slithered in and gave a salute much crisper than mine, which, considering she was a snake, was rather impressive. "Sorry. Just out. Another Snowy from the tree across just took flight and is heading toward the Point. Guess young Moss has set a new standard."

Would this never stop? Everyone except yours truly here seemed to be progressing in the speediest manner — fever speed! — toward true flight and Dark Fowl Island. And now most frustrating of all, we were off to visit Moss's hollow. The new local hero in flight accomplishments. I would probably make a mess of even this brief flight, which, truth be told, wasn't more than extended branching.

Mum and Da went out on a brief hunting foray. They said it was gracious when visiting neighbors to bring a rodent. I could hear Gilda's swishings as she slithered about, swiping up vermin with her forked tongue and neatening the hollow. I watched as Mum and Da lofted themselves onto a gust. Wings spread, they carved tight elegant turns until they were over the crowns of the trees that made up our small grove. They angled their wings so the tips seemed to brush the sky. *I envy them; if I could only fly so beautifully.*

"So do I," a voice behind me spoke softly.

"Gilda!" I wheeled about, nearly losing my balance on the rim of the hollow. I thought the words were in my head, but I must have whispered them aloud.

"Yes. Your parents are beautiful fliers. It stirs me deeply."

I blinked. Gilda had twisted herself into a neat coil and had been peering over my shoulder out into the night, tracking my parents' flight.

"But how can you envy them? You're a snake."

"I know. Odd, isn't it? But I can just imagine what it might feel like to fly."

"You can?"

"Yes," she answered with a wistfulness to her voice as she gazed out the hollow.

I looked at her as she slithered off. Something struck me about this snake. Mrs. Grinkle was nice, but Gilda was much more interesting. I was drawn to her from the time she first arrived, for some reason. I think it was her stories — she told the best twixt-time stories as the dawn came and I was supposed to be settling down to sleep. But now I knew what it really was that captivated me. It was her imagination. Any snake who could imagine flying had to be special in some way. That's probably why Gilda wasn't a very good nest-maid. She thought deeply and didn't pay attention to bark worms and wood beetles and such.

I followed Gilda back into the deepest part of the hollow, where she was wrestling with a small nest of thread worms.

"What'cha want, dearie?" She turned around.

I just blurted it out. "I'm scared that I'll make a mess of landing on that branch outside of Moss's hollow and everyone will laugh at me. Everyone flies so much better than I do."

"Oh, nonsense, Lyze. You'll do just fine."

"No, I won't!"

"You won't if you say you won't. You must believe you will, lad."

"But how can I believe I will if I am . . . am . . . am . . ."

"Not sure?"

"Yes. Not sure. How do you believe if you're not sure?"

"Now that is a good question. Some creatures say faith is believing what you cannot see or prove. But I believe that faith is the power to imagine. If you can imagine the feel of the air beneath your wings, if you can picture in your mind's eye your plummels[4] brushing the sounds from the night and quieting your passage, then you will fly as a well as any owl."

Gilda was right, so right!

"My goodness," Mum gasped as I landed on the branch.

"I've never seen anything like it!" my father said, his voice tinged with awe. "You flew as if every single one of your plummels had budged and they haven't yet, have they? They're always the last to come."

"No, I don't think they have," I replied.

"Then how did you do it? You were so quiet," Mum asked.

"Oh, I just imagined the plummels."

"Imagined?" Both my parents said the word at once, as if they had never heard it before.

---

4   Plummels are the fringe feathers that line the outer edges of most owls' wings. They are responsible for making us the quietest flyers on Earth. Plummels are made of the most delicate filaments of feathers.

Moss's hollow was at least twice as large as ours. This was to be expected, I suppose, seeing as Snowies are more than twice the size of Whiskered Screeches. From their heads to their tails, they measure the length of three Screeches, end to end. But the thing I remember best is how wilfed Moss was. He was all scrunched up at his mum's legs like a chick trying to get warm under her belly feathers. This was Moss? The gifted, talented Moss? I was astounded. But I had forgotten how I had seen him wilf the day his mum first arrived. Now he seemed not just puny, but frightened and scared. Yes, frightened! The mighty Moss, who just a few nights before had returned from his triumphant circumnavigation of the Hock! What was wrong with him? He seemed to be cowering, and every time his mum moved, so did he. It was as if he couldn't be an inch from her. Was Moss a mama's owlet?

The visit started out with the requisite small talk. Profuse thanks for the two voles my parents had brought, more talk about Moss's amazing circumnavigation, but then as always, the conversation turned to the war.

"Yes, Hrenna had a time of it up around Little Hoole."

"They have a few small stealth units wreaking havoc up there. They hide out in the fissures."

"Snow leopard terrain," my father said. I was immediately alert. Snow leopards had fascinated me, and Gilda had once told me a twixt-time story about them. They could not be found as far south as Stormfast and lived in the high mountain ranges above the H'rathghar glacier. Fierce, with fangs nearly as long and sharp as ice scimitars, and exceedingly swift, they were, my father said, "Built to kill." There was a pause in the conversation as Hrenna and Arne, her mate, exchanged glances. Arne gave her a barely perceptible nod, and I noticed Moss begin to quiver.

"Yes, built to kill," Arne said.

Then Hrenna spoke in a rasping whisper. "And so am I!" She lifted her port leg. The foot was blackened and the four talons fused together into one mangled lump. I must have looked shocked, for she turned to me and then to Moss. "Don't fret," she said cheerfully. "You're never really tested until you're in the field of battle, and you young'uns will both make wonderful soldiers. I know it! Don't you, Rask? Don't you, Ulfa?"

I had to fight hard now not to wilf in front of everyone's eyes. I noticed that Moss didn't look too chipper, either, which made me feel a tad better.

"It wasn't the snow leopards that got me, though. It was two Eagle Owls. They thought they had me when they came at me with a fizblister. . . ."

The grown-ups kept talking, but Moss was wilfing so fiercely I thought he might simply vanish. Now I understood. He was overwhelmed with shame! Yes, shame at the hideous deformity of his mum's talons and how they looked as if they had melted in the fires of hagsmire. The grown-ups were consumed with talk of war and not paying a bit of attention to us.

"This foot has become a weapon in its own right. I swear it's as powerful as one of those gigantic snow leopard paws. The force I can deliver with it is amazing. After I healed and was battle ready again, I managed to crack one of the enemy Eagle Owl's starboard wings nearly in two in an ambush half a moon later." She raised the foot with the fused, blackened talons. It looked like a club.

"An Eagle Owl!" I heard my parents exclaim. An Eagle Owl had a wingspan at least half again as big as a Snowy's.

She chuckled a bit. "Now I lead a commando unit called the Flying Leopards. Did it with this! It's better than an ice ax. One might say this wound has made me 'built to kill.'" Hrenna shook the mangled talon.

Moss had clamped his eyes shut. It was clear that he was a bundle of fear and shame. I lofted myself into the dim light of the hollow and flew toward my mum.

"What is it?" she asked. I gave a small tug on her bandanna. "Oh, my, you want me to show off my battle scar, do you?" She chuckled, obviously pleased. "It's not a competition, you know, dear. Hrenna and I both did our bit. That's all a soldier can do." No, it wasn't a competition, but how could I explain that to Mum? I just wanted Moss to see that I knew what he had been feeling.

Moss sidled up to me and whispered, "I saw you arrive tonight. It was a beautiful landing. Better than any I've ever made. How soon do you think you might be ready for Dark Fowl?"

"I'm not sure. Why?"

"Because I'd like to fly there with you. It would be much more fun if we could go together."

So it was on that night, in the hollow of the Snowies while our mums and das spoke of war and bloody battles, that Moss and I became best friends.

CHAPTER 5

A Snake Named Hoke

Shortly after our visit with Moss's family, I attained that most significant flight mark for an owlet before going to Dark Fowl. I made my own trip to the Hock. Da was there to coach me but I already had a feel for the breezes and knew when to sheer off a boisterous draft. That evening, I soared for the first time. I seemed to have an instinct for the warm thermal updrafts, and what a thrill those silken billows of warm air were to ride! I didn't even have to flap my wings once and yet I slid effortlessly through the starry night. As I soared, I could not help but think of Gilda. Her words about faith came back to me, about believing in what you cannot see.

Yes, I was flying, but I was experiencing something more than that on this beautiful night. Another kind of faith began to seep into my mind and as I flipped my head back to look at the star-dusted sky, I thought I could almost see the face of Glaux.

"Hock ho!" My da's call split the night and then I saw it. The steep cliff that climbed out of the sea.

"What's that?" I called back.

"What's what?" Just off the cliff, the night was laced with iridescent threads of turquoise and greenish light. "Oh, yes, of course! Always a surprise the first time you see them. Diving snakes."

"Great Glaux, snakes can fly?" I thought of Gilda immediately.

"Oh, no! No, never. They can swim, though, and they dive into the sea from their caves."

My beak dropped open in amazement. I could never have imagined anything like this. "B-b-bu — b-bu — but how do they get back up the cliff again?"

"They crawl up, same way they slither up our trees in the grove."

"But where do they live?"

"In the cliffs. They find nooks and crannies, and they burrow out others. Let me tell you, there is nothing stronger than a Kielian snake. And you'll see when we go to Dark Fowl — their fangs. They use them to hone the edges of the ice scimitars."

"But Gilda and Mrs. Grinkle, they're Kielian snakes. I've never seen their fangs."

"Well, they keep them tucked away. Not much use for them in domestic service, really."

"Can we visit the Hock snakes? I want to meet some."

"Whatever for, lad?" Da looked absolutely dumbfounded. My facial feathers must have wilfed with disappointment, because he continued, "Well, I suppose it would be all right. But you know, they aren't all that sociable. They don't like company."

"Will they bite me?"

"Oh, no! They're not aggressive. They just like to keep to themselves, especially the ones on Hock. There's a reason why they seek out the most Glaux-forsaken place on Stormfast. They like the isolation. I — I —" he stammered. I don't think I had ever heard my da stammer but he seemed totally bewildered by me. He collected himself and started again. "I mean, say again why you want to meet them?"

"I'm just interested, that's all. Another species, you know. Just curious." How does one explain curiosity? "Uh — what if I just sort of went up and said hello?"

"I suppose so. The worst that could happen is that they wouldn't say hello back," my da said doubtfully.

That was all I had to hear. I was determined to meet a Kielian snake — and not one who worked as a nest-maid for my family. So, like Moss, we began a circumnavigation of the Hock. I didn't just go around it, but scoured its entire vertical surface looking for a friendly face. There were indeed many faces — hundreds of them rose from the tumultuous sea and began their long, slow slither up the sheer cliff to the top where they could dive off again. The moon had begun to set, and their iridescent scales sparkled even more brightly in the darkening sky.

I tried saying hello and good evening to dozens of snakes while they whizzed by me on the plunge toward the sea. I said, "Gundin hagen" or just a quick "hagen" or sometimes "hagen, hordo." "Hordo" was the Krakish word for "snake." I assumed they spoke Krakish, the language of the Northern Kingdoms, and not some kind of snake language. I mean Gilda and Mrs. Grinkle spoke Krakish fluently. Surely, these snakes did even if they were unsociable. I began working the midsection of the cliffs more diligently, as there were a few crannies in which I could see the twinkling glimmer of scales.

"Hagen, hordo," I said to a snake who poked his head out.

The snake whipped his head around. "Evening, snake?" he replied incredulously. "I know I'm a snake. I don't need it confirmed by you. I mean, I don't say 'good evening, bird.'"

"Well, I'm not just a bird, I'm an owl — a Whiskered Screech to be precise."

"And I am not just a snake, but a Kielian snake, a spotted azure-back to be precise."

"Uh . . . what's azure?"

"What's azure? Are you serious? You don't know what azure is?"

"If I were a snake, maybe I would."

"If you were a snake . . ." he sneered. His eyes seemed not to blink exactly but slide with a glittering flash and then simply vanish. I would later learn that snakes do not have three eyelids as owls do — upper, lower, and then the wiper membrane — but only one, if indeed you could call it an eyelid at all. Their eyelids are composed of transparent scales that close either vertically or horizontally. There was a second flash and the snake's eyes were back. The snake seemed to have gone through an odd transformation, almost a molting, not of his skin but of his attitude.

"I shall attempt to be patient." The sneer was gone. It was not as if this snake had become all warm and fuzzy; it's very hard to be warm and fuzzy if one is an elongated, legless creature with scales.

"Hoke's the name," the snake said.

"I thought this place was called Hock?" I asked.

"Me, idiot." The eyes flashed again. "My name is Hoke. Hoke of Hock." The sneer had returned. His voice seemed to curdle with contempt.

I was catching on. I could play his game, too. "Ah, I see! You're trying to tell me you're an idiot," I parried. His mouth cracked open and he flung back his head, exposing the longest, sharpest fangs one might ever imagine, and croaked — not hissed, mind you, but croaked — this was how Kielian snakes laugh. But did I know he was laughing? I did not. I was scared out of my gizzard and began to back out of the cranny, nearly falling off the ledge before I could spread my wings.

"Come back! Come back!" he hissed. "I like you. You made me laugh."

Let me just say this: When a Hoolian snake laughs, it can scare you to death. But I returned, for despite the laugh, there was a kindness in Hoke's voice.

"Come in, come in. Make yourself at home," he said with real warmth. "My nost." He swung his head about. The "nost" was what Kielian snakes called their hollows, and this nost was much larger than I had anticipated.

"Do you live here by yourself?"

"No, my parents are off visiting relatives. My sisters and brothers are around someplace. Probably still diving."

I looked about. "I didn't realize these cliff nosts were so large."

"They aren't. We make them that way. We dig and tunnel with our fangs and heads."

"I've never understood that." I tried to picture Mrs. Grinkle digging through what appeared to be solid rock.

"No, you wouldn't," he said with a slight sneer, but I decided to let it pass.

"Why not?"

"Well, you've probably only been exposed to nest-maid snakes."

"True."

"And nest-maids really only need their tongues for vermin slurping, and their heads for whisking up dust and twigs and all matter of debris that litter owl hollows. 'Tidy butts' we call them."

"But you're snakes. You don't have butts."

"No kidding!" A smirk scrolled across his face. "Sometimes we borrow a little bit of language from other species, particularly body-part words. Try being legless, wingless, long, and tubular. We are not spineless, however. What a relief!"

"But even so, you dig through rock. How?"

To answer my question, the snake called Hoke began the most astounding sequence of shape-shifting acts imaginable.

"Well," he said as his head flattened into a thick wedge with a new set of scales beginning to fringe the edges. "You've seen this, of course, in your nest-maids. The basic whisking or broom phase for cleaning owl hollows." In truth, I had never really paid attention when Mrs. Grinkle or Gilda swept up. But they did have a secondary set of scales that seemed to gather around their necks, if indeed those long, wingless bodies had necks. "But have you seen this?" Hoke's head swelled into a large, bulbous configuration. "Great for smashing lithite — that's the kind of rock these cliffs are made of. Let me demonstrate." There was a small chunk of rock nearby. "Watch this. Please note, I do a semi coil, as it gives me the right amount of heft for this size rock. A-one, and a-two, and a-three!" Within seconds, the rock had been reduced to smithereens, and a small dusting of scales drifted down among the chips. "Not to worry. The scales regenerate quickly. The rock doesn't, however."

Something slithered in the rear of the nost. There was a yawn and a childlike voice called, "Why did you wake me up?"

"Hellie, that you?"

"Yeah! Who else? You're supposed to be snake-sitting me, remember? And instead, you're just showing off." A tiny little snake wriggled toward the shattered rock. "Great Hordox,[5] you're talking to an owl."

Hellie was almost the same color as Hoke, but somewhat paler.

"Is she also a spotted azure-back?" I asked.

"Of course I am. I'm his sister!" She opened her mouth quite wide to announce this, and despite her small size, she had formidable fangs.

"Now you're showing off," Hoke said. "She just dropped her baby fangs last night and these new ones came in today."

"I am not!" she replied huffily.

---

[5]   Hordox, I was to learn, was the serpent spirit. There is also a constellation called Hordox that appears briefly at the end of the summer moons. Oddly enough, the Kielian snakes were mostly oblivious to this constellation, which I must assume is due to the fact that they don't fly.

"Just answer me one thing," I said. "You never explained what 'azure' is. It's a word I've never heard."

"It's a color!" Hellie squawked.

"Be patient, Hellie. He's only an owl."

"Duh!" she muttered.

Only, I thought, but let it pass.

Hoke swung his head toward me. "Azure is a shade of blue. It is closer to the color of the sky on a clear, cloudless day. But then there is cyan and cerulean — very close to azure and then cerulean lazuli and then turquoise and cobalt and violusia. And with the violusians, you have both your striated and your non-striated. The striated tend more toward the deep purple, the non-striated are more or less lavender. You see, there are over a thousand shades of blue for Kielian snakes. Our scales are actually a spectrum of all of these shades, but some of us are more azure while some tip toward the purple end of the spectrum."[6]

I was almost dizzy from the recitation of the blue spectrum of Kielian snake colors.

"Did you show him your shim head? Do it!" Hellie urged. It was apparent that she was much more interested in her brother's

---

[6] I would later write a book *One Thousand Shades of Blue: An Analysis of the Spectral Coordinates of Kielian Snakes*. It was considered a seminal work in spectroscopic studies.

ability to reconfigure his head shape than in a discussion of colors.

"Would you like to try it, Hellie?" Hoke asked gently.

"Oh, I can't do it like you can."

"Try." He turned to me. "Hellie is just developing her head-shaping muscles. The more she practices, the better she'll get."

"All right. I'll try but don't expect too much."

"Remember, concentrate," Hoke urged.

Hellie uncoiled her entire body and made herself as flat as possible on the floor of the nost. She grew very still. "I'm concentrating," she whispered. Her eyes seemed to cross with the effort. I noticed a quiver in her head. It was flattening slowly into a spade shape.

"Good, good, you've got the shape!"

"But I can't get it thin enough!" she cried in exasperation. Her body suddenly contracted, and she recoiled herself. "It's not a shim, it's a big, fat, old lumpy thing," she whined.

"You had the shape, Hellie, you really did!" Hoke said.

"You show him how it's supposed to be done."

Within seconds, Hoke was stretched out to his full length, and his head was as thin as a wet leaf and very rigid. He slithered over to two rocks that were stacked atop each other in a notch in the wall and began prying at the bottom one. "With a shim-shaped head, it's amazing what one can do."

"What's amazing," Hellie whispered, clearly entranced by

her brother's abilities, "is that he can do this while he is talking and not lose his head shape." Within seconds, the bottom rock was free. With Hellie's encouragement, Hoke went on to demonstrate another half dozen head shapes he had mastered — the sledgehammer, the anvil, the ax, and so on.

I heard a flapping of wings outside the nost. "Lyze! Lyze! You in there?"

"Oh, Da, yes. Sorry."

"Lyze?" Hoke said. "Is that your name?"

"Yes. I'm sorry I never properly introduced myself."

My father stuck his head inside. He blinked with surprise.

"Da, meet my friend Hoke and his little sister Hellie."

"Well . . . well . . . I'll be!" Da said.

CHAPTER 6

Sea Smoke

"Well, I'll be . . . I'll be," my da kept muttering as we flew back in the breaking light of the dawn. It was a beautiful flight — the sky was tinted with an earthly pink and, just above, a soft blue began to show. Was it azure? Cerulean? Cyan? Then a low mist started to roll across the choppy waters of the Everwinter Sea.

"What is that?" I asked my father, nodding down at the water.

"Sea smoke."

"Sea smoke? Is there a fire someplace?"

"No, lad. Some call it 'sea steam.'"

"What causes it?"

"Ah, you're a curious one, aren't you, lad? I like that. Well, it's caused when very cold air moves in over warmer water. The water on the surface begins to evaporate and that's about all I can tell you."

That was enough to get me thinking. "Da, can I fly down there and skim the surface? I want to see this sea smoke close up."

"As long as you don't get lost in it. You be careful. If it starts to close in on you, fly back up here right away."

My father was a bit anxious, but he was not one to stand in the way of a young and inquiring mind. So I began a steeply banking turn. I could almost feel his eyes boring into me. I was careful to angle my wings just so, in what I felt was the stylish manner that he and Mum did when they made a steep descent to our tree. Until that moment, I thought this wing tilt was dashing, but now I realized that it was very useful for sensing the different layers of air.

Just above the sea smoke, the layer of air was cool, but closer to the water, it was much warmer. Odd, I had never thought of the Everwinter Sea as feeling warm. But I realized that it was warm only in comparison to the cold air sweeping down from the north. *That must be glacier air,* I thought. The droplets of moisture in the sea smoke were large and I was becoming quite damp. My primaries were growing heavier with the accumulated moisture. *Well,* I thought, *I'll just have to stroke a little bit harder.* I felt a twinge in my gizzard as I realized that visibility was shutting down. Just then, I heard the sonorous alarm call of my da. I had done exactly what he said not to do, gotten lost in the sea smoke.

Fear was quickly getting the best of me. I felt it flood through my hollow bones. Something peculiar was happening to my primaries. *Oh, no. Kerplonken! I'm going kerplonken.*

Just fledged, first real flight, and I go kerplonken.[7] The sea smoke was swirling all around me. Which way was up? Which way was down? If I didn't do something soon, I'd hit the water's surface and drown.

Then it occurred to me; up had to be drier because the air above the sea smoke would be drier than the air closest to the sea. My da's words came back to me: *Very cold air moves in over warmer water. The water on the surface begins to evaporate.* So the air would not only be drier, but colder. If I couldn't see, I must feel my way back to safety. I stuck a talon straight out in one direction and the other in the opposite. My starboard talon felt slightly drier. I power-flapped both wings. The tips of my primaries were gripping the chill air. To tell you the truth, I didn't know if I was flying or clawing my way out of the sea smoke, but somehow I made it.

My father emitted a long, low hoot — a hoot of both relief and anguish. He grabbed me by his talons and yanked me up higher.

"I can fly, Da. I can fly now. I'm all right."

"I know you're all right, lad, I know it. And Glaux knows you can fly. Never seen anything like it. You were clambering out of that sea smoke as if you were half owl and half . . .

---

7   "Kerplonken" is Krakish for the perhaps more familiar Hoolian word "yeep," which means "wing locked."

half . . . I don't know! A snow leopard scaling the highest peaks of the H'rathghar glacier. Let's go home now."

My father paused for a moment, an odd expression crossing his face.

"And, Lyze," he added, "let's keep this little adventure between the two of us. Don't mention anything to your mum. It's not a good time to upset her."

We did not get home until well after twixt time. But as soon as we entered the hollow, I knew something was different. One could just feel it. Da twitched a wing tip to signal me to be quiet and then nodded and led me over to where Mum was settled on a tumble of rabbit's ear moss and peels of birch bark. It sort of looked like a nest, but not quite. There was more down poking out from the sides.

"Why is Mum sleeping there? What is that thing?" I asked.

Da churred softly. "How quickly you forget."

"Forget what?" Slowly, the pellet dropped, as the expression goes. This wasn't just any nest. It was an egg nest, a brooding nest. Mum had laid an egg.

"C'mon. Crouch down a bit, and we might be able to get a glimpse of it."

I crouched down next to Da, full of all sorts of excited little feelings. My gizzard was hopping around like a bark beetle. I saw just a bit of something white — creamy white. *That must be it!* I thought. My *little brother . . . or sister.*

"Does it have wings yet? A beak? Legs?"

"Give it time, lad. It's got a lot of growing to do."

CHAPTER 7

Ice Dagger

"Can you believe it, Lyze? Tonight's the night!"

What I really couldn't believe was that Moss had actually delayed his first flight to Dark Fowl to wait for me. He wanted us to fly together. But as I was standing on that branch, a wind began to blow. Something about it caught my attention. There was a low whine at its edges and, every now and then, almost a gasp.

"Hey, Lyze, what's wrong? Bad pellet?" Moss hooted softly. I was wilfing before his eyes.

"No, no, Moss," I said, looking up at him. "I don't think we should go tonight."

"What? What are you saying? Not go?! Lyze, this is what we have been waiting for forever! Going to Dark Fowl! Meeting Orf and his smiths."

But I told him I wouldn't and returned home.

My parents must have sensed something was wrong as soon as I entered the hollow.

"By Glaux, lad, looks like you've seen a scroom!"

"Not seen. Heard."

"Heard? Heard what?" Da asked.

"Out there, the wind suddenly shifted and it seemed to die. At first, it sounded like a mewling, like a baby animal . . . weak, frightened . . . and . . . and dying." Both my parents gasped in horror.

"I told you he had a feel for weather, Ulfa." Da flipped his head around sharply at Mum, then back to me.

"It ain't a baby, ain't no chick, no cub," my father said. "You might as well ram a hot blade through your gizzard. It's the Snurls, and we ain't flyin' tonight."

"The Snurls?" I asked. The Shagdah Snurl was far to the north and was said to be the hatching place of the winds. Legend had it that the winds were caused by two battling sisters whose fight raked the Northern Kingdoms. Mum said legends sometimes made things more understandable. She said some owls needed stories to explain things beyond their control. "Some things," she said, "are beyond what we can feel in our gizzards, know in our hearts, or can reason in our brains." But now it began to feel as if the Snurl sisters had arrived at our hollow. For, by midnight, the rasp I'd heard had grown into a snarl and there was a terrible shaking of the tree. The very bark seemed to quiver.

"Don't worry," Mum said from her perch on the nest. "We're very safe here." But I noticed that Gilda had wrapped herself around the base of the egg nest. "We must remain calm." My mother adjusted her bandanna and sat erect on the nest. To me, she was not just a mum guarding her nest, but a commando heading into battle.

"Don't worry, dear. The tree won't break. That is why Da and I chose this pine. It's young and full of sap. A tree with sap doesn't break. It bends with the wind, but never splinters." But at that moment, the tree seemed to moan and I felt our hollow tip slightly. "It won't break, I promise you,"[8] Mum said, and reached out a talon to pat me.

And for the rest of the night, she told me stories about the Shagdah Snurl, this incredible place that was part legend but part real, where rocks melted, sisters squabbled, and the winds hatched. I was mesmerized.

By the next evening, our world in the grove was calm. The winds had subsided and we were ready to fly to Dark Fowl. Mum let Gundesfyrr sit on the nest so she could see us take off. From the neighboring pine, a family of Sooty Owls perched to wave good-bye and, of course, across the way, Moss's family had gathered on the large branch outside their hollow. I always felt it was quite beautiful when Moss and his da, Arne, spread their

---

8   I would later learn that although a pine was in fact the safest place to be during a Snurl gale, it was the last tree one wanted to be in during a forest fire. As the flames burn, the sap begins to boil, and the tree can explode in a matter of minutes.

lovely white wings, but at this moment I felt my wings, though smaller, were equally beautiful with their mottling of brown and gray and tawny feathers with accents of white.

My heart was pounding and my gizzard a-jitter. I had been too excited to eat and, besides, I wanted to fly light. It was as if every feather, right down to my plummels, was anticipating each wind riffle and draft it might encounter. I wanted to embrace the wind, the sky, the very stars. How lucky I was to have been born a bird, and not just any bird, but an owl! For what other creature can fly with such grace, carve the wind with such elegance, and pass through the air in utter silence?

Regard the map and you will see that between Stormfast Island and Dark Fowl there is another island, the Ice Dagger. I had studied that map the previous morning until Mum made me go to sleep. Now, with the wind coming in from the southeast, we had to take a quartering tack and fly several degrees off the shortest route, which took us directly over the Dagger. A tailwind would have made everything much easier, but Moss and I were ecstatic. For the Dagger was where the ice was harvested for the premier ice weapons — those used by the Frost Beaks, the Ice Lancers, the Ice Squires, and all the elite ice regiments of the Kielian League. As we flew over the Point of Hock, I scanned the cliffs for Hoke, but there was no sign of him. I was determined to meet up with him again.

Not long after, my father flipped his head back, twisting it as only owls can due to the extra bones in their necks that allow us to swivel in a wider arc than any other creature. My father had not only twisted his head back, but flipped it entirely upside down. "Young'uns, you can catch your first glimpse of some harvesters near the point of the Dagger."

We saw them immediately: two Short-eared Owls and a Barn Owl hovering in the air.

Our fathers began to talk about the harvesting blades they were using. "I think the Barn Owl is using a tactical planar blade while the two Short-ears are working with the standard ice chisel," Da said. "Arne, how about we take the lads in for a close-up view?"

Moss and I were beside ourselves and started to hoot with joy.

"Now, lads!" My father turned to us. "None of that. Ice harvesting is serious business. One slip of the blade can be disastrous. We have to hang back and let these owls concentrate. When they finish their business, they might take a break and talk to us. But be quiet for now."

Arnc added, "Do nothing to distract them."

A warm thermal conveniently rose out of nowhere so that we could soar quietly above the harvesters and observe their work. These owls were not simply magnificent fliers who did complex wing work to keep close to the blade of the Ice Dagger, but they were master craftsmen. Below the harvesters, two more Short-ears and a Barn Owl flew with what looked like slings suspended from their talons.

"Scrappers," my father whispered.

"Huh?"

"The ones with the slings. They're apprentices to the ice harvesters. Their main job is to collect the shards as the masters sheer them off. See how carefully they watch for when a shard is about to break off?"

My gizzard quivered with excitement. I wanted to be a scrapper. How much one could learn!

Something caught my father's attention. The first thread of a newing moon glimmered behind the scrim of dark scudding clouds. Suddenly, there was a sound I had never heard — a sizzling scratch in the air. Sparks flew and blood splattered the night. For a brief instant, it was as if we were all frozen in a crimson rain. And then I saw a wingless Short-eared Owl plummet toward the sea.

"It's an attack!" the Barn Owl cried. He drew an ice shard from the sling his scrapper carried.

"Quick! To the ledge, lads!" Da shrieked. *What ledge?* I looked down at the sharp vertical blade of the ice cliff beneath me, shimmering in the night.

"Behind the blade on the other side!" Arne rasped. They herded us to the far side of the island.

"Who are they?" Moss asked.

I could see the disbelief in both our fathers' eyes. "Hireclaws for the Ice Talons League? B-but — but —" my da stammered. "How could this be?"

Arne swiveled his head around madly. "They've never come this far west, this far into civilian air — and — and territory. This is so far from the front!"

"Or what we thought was the front," my father said ominously.

"You lads stay here," Arne replied. There was a distinct alarm in the Snowy's eyes. This was not how our first flight to Dark Fowl was supposed to go. Not at all.

"What are you going to do?" Moss asked. "You and Rask don't have weapons!"

"Yes, you do!" It was the shree of the Barn Owl scrapper, who plunged in with his sling. "Take an ice shard, you two. They're not finished, but they'll work. Let the owlets take these ice hooks. Don't use them until you have to," the Barn Owl said. "You toss the hooks. First power up and then lob them. You've played lob and gob, haven't you?" We both nodded. "Same idea."

He was off before we could ask any more questions.

Da looked at us. "Stay here. Don't move. Be alert and you'll be safe." He swallowed. "Don't use those weapons unless you absolutely have to."

And then they were gone. Thick clouds rolled in, making it harder to see. We heard terrible screeches tearing the night. The shree of a Barn Owl is one of the most gizzard-shattering sounds on Earth. But were our Barn Owls, the harvester and his scrapper, being torn to pieces or was it a war whoop? Feathers drifted lazily through the darkness. It was impossible to tell to whom they belonged: a Short-eared Owl or a Barn Owl or — and these we dreaded seeing the most — the pure white feathers of a Snowy or the mottled brown-gray ones of a Whiskered Screech.

Suddenly, a white face rimmed with tawny feathers appeared out of the clouds just below the ledge, shooting up toward us. There was a strange mark between its eyes, bloodred, but not made from blood, a double crescent shape that talons make when tearing flesh. I realized it had been painted with a stain extracted from bingle berries. It had a terrifying impact on me, for there was something almost hypnotic about the design.

The owl raised talons sheathed in metal. I heard the click of his battle claws extending and smelled the rank odor of day-old vole on his breath as his beak dropped open to screech the kill chant. The claws were a whisker's breadth from my ear slit, set to rake off half my face.

Moss and I leaped into the air. I heard the sound of those claws raking the ledge where I was perched just a second before and then a terrible sizzle as if something hot had touched the ice. I flipped my head around. The owl was coming at me, the double extension talon on his battle claws reaching for me. And they were fire claws. Their tips glowed like the eyes of a hagsfiend, and I could feel the radiating heat on my tail feathers. If he touched me, I would ignite like a ball of fire.

The Barn Owl was chasing us. The ice hook was heavier than I thought and my flight balance was off. I wobbled a bit at first, then recovered. A few seconds later, I sensed a new wind in my feathers. It was what I can best describe as a "curling gust." Whiskered Screeches are small owls. What we lack in raw power, we make up for in agility. How I felt I could do this I am not sure, but I flipped myself over on that curl of wind so that I was flying upside down, or rather belly up, cradled in the gutter of a sustained gust.[7] Above me, I could see the flash of the Barn Owl's battle claws in the night. My gizzard nearly seized up because he was directly above me, but he seemed not to realize it.

---

7   In my future weather studies, I would do extensive research on the architectural structure of the winds of gales, storms, hurricanes, and typhoons. "Gutter" is a term often used to describe the edging troughs of a variety of winds. My book *Scuppers, Gutters, and Baggywrinkles: The Architecture of Storms* became required reading for all members of the weather-interpretation chaw at the Great Ga'Hoole Tree.

The soft white feathers of his belly gleamed. The peculiar markings I had seen on his face, the double crescent, haunted me still. I had no battle claws. I had the hook, but it wasn't the best weapon for what I was hoping to do. But my talons were sharp. Suppose I clawed him? Without thinking any further, I thrust both my talons up at once. The impact wasn't much, but the shock was huge. The Barn Owl squawked and tipped precariously. I saw something slice through the night, and the Barn Owl lurched. Moss's ice hook had fastened onto his port battle claws. Moss had him tethered, and his belly was bleeding from where I had clawed him.

"You got him!" It was Arne, Moss's father, crying out. Blood coursed down one of his own wings, but he was flying steadily. Then my father and two of the harvesters appeared. The Short-eared harvester plunged toward the hireclaw Barn Owl with an immense ice shard and stabbed him in the belly to finish him off.

He flew back, pointing. "We'll fetch up on the Dagger," said the harvester.

We flew to a narrow rocky beach on the lee side of the Ice Dagger. There were nine of us in all. The Short-eared harvester, a female named Aiyunne, extended a wing and patted her scrapper, Bela, who was sobbing. The only time I had ever seen a grown-up crying was when I was hatched out, and the messenger came and told of Edvard's death. And though I didn't know the owl who had died, my eyes also filled with tears.

Moss was trembling. "Wh . . . what . . ." Before he got the words out, I knew what he was going to ask. "What were those marks, those red marks on their faces?"

"Ah!" Arne sighed deeply.

"The double crescent — an ancient Krakish symbol, evoking Bhachtyr."

"Bhachtyr?" Moss and I both said at once.

"The Sacred Force from ancient times — Bhachtyr the Destroyer. Bylyric has taken this as his symbol. Sometimes they have a strange effect. We're used to seeing it, but the first time it's hard. Rough on the gizzard."

Aiyunne, the Short-eared harvester, gave a muffled sob. Her scrapper turned to her. "I'm so sorry about Piet."

"He's down there someplace, isn't he? He can't even have a proper burial!"[10]

---

10 A proper burial for a dead owl in the Northern Kingdoms consisted of burning the owl and then setting out the ashes on a sea wind. In the Southern Kingdoms, an owl's body is transported to a high hollow in a pepper-gum tree, safe from scavengers, or can also be burned. Owls of the Southern Kingdoms are not particular about where or what kind of wind they release the ashes upon. I have made a codicil in my will that my ashes shall be transported to the Northern Kingdoms, preferably near the Bay of Fangs, for private reasons that I do not wish to disclose.

"Is — is —" I began stuttering.

"What, son?" My da turned to me.

"Never mind," I replied in a small voice.

I was going to ask if the owl, the owl I had never even met, was really dead. But I knew that was stupid, childish. I kept peering down into the tumult of the Everwinter Sea expecting to see the owl emerge. How could someone be here one minute and gone the next? I had to stop myself from saying the dumbest thing of all, the most babyish thing of all: *no fair!* Can you imagine ever hearing a soldier, a warrior, cry "no fair"? The order of the universe had gone yoickers.

CHAPTER 8

A Place of Fire and Song

We flew at a blistering pace to Dark Fowl. There was simply no time to waste. The attack on the Ice Dagger was the farthest west an Ice Talon unit had come into Kielian League territory; indeed, it was close to the very heart of our territory. Both my father and Arne thought they recognized one of the attacking owls as Bylyric's top lieutenant. I flew even faster when I heard them say this. It was almost as if I could feel the shadow of the Orphan Maker on my tail feathers, blotting out the stars, the moon, making the dark feel even blacker. My father and Arne were flying directly to General Andricus Tyto Alba at command headquarters to report the attack to him.

As we approached Dark Fowl, the wind brought the acrid smell of the forges and a few tentacles of dark smoke scrolled across the sky. We went into wide, banking turns, and our fathers led Moss and me on a low flight so we could see the lay of the island. The flames from two dozen or more forges licked the twilight like bright red tongues.

There is no place quite like Dark Fowl Island. It is a place of fire and song, slogs and smiths, forges and training fields. Security is tight, for this is the place where weapons are not just wrought out of metal and ice, but invented. Of all the places in the owl world, this one came closest to what the Others would call a city. It bustled with scrappers and harvesters, Kielian snakes who honed the blades of scimitars and ice swords with their fangs, young cadets beginning their military training. You must imagine what this was like for Moss and me. Neither one of us had seen much more than the immediate neighborhood of our own respective trees until we made our first flights to Hock. Stormfast was not a heavily populated island, particularly the region where we lived. I had never even met a Short-eared or a Barn Owl until we encountered harvesters and scrappers on the Ice Dagger.

"I see old Garn must be using caribou droppings," Da said.

"Caribou droppings?" Moss and I both asked at once.

"What's a caribou, Da?" I asked.

"A four leg."

"Four leg!" we blurted out in unison. We had heard of four legs, but never seen one.

"They don't live around here, that's for sure," my da said. "Garn had to go all the way to the Beyond for that. Getting pretty old for such a long flight."

"Look at the forge down to port. Smell it." Owls are not known for their olfactory abilities, but I could smell something that seemed to hint of the sea. "Fish oil and well-seasoned seaweed. It's Juhani's forge. He's a Fish Owl," Arne explained.

Our fathers had to go directly to command headquarters, so they arranged for Juhani's assistant, an Elf Owl, to take us about. His name was Rolf, and he was an old friend of Da's from his family hollow in Squeeze-Through-Tickle in the Tridents. Da and Arne would meet us later at Orf's forge. We were both eager to see Orf's forge, for if any island had a king, Orf was definitely the monarch of Dark Fowl. Even in his long, distinguished ancestry of blacksmiths, it was said Orf was the very best.

"Orf's forge is actually smaller than any of the others that you've seen," Rolf said as we followed him. "It always surprises owls."

"It surprises me," Moss said. "I mean, he's the most famous, yet he has the smallest forge. How come?"

"It's his way. He's a modest sort. Doesn't like a lot of owls fussing around. Only has one apprentice while most master smiths have three or four," Rolf explained. "Now, look down to starboard. The barracks are in that outcropping of lithite rocks. That's where you'll stay when you become cadets."

Cadets. The word had a magic ring. But it would be several moons before we were grown enough to become cadets. I began to wonder if the only thing cadets learned was how to fight. "Are there other kinds of cadets?" I asked.

My father and Arne flew in and caught my question. "What are you talking about, son?" Da looked utterly bewildered.

"I'm — I'm not sure. I mean, do you learn other things than just fighting?"

"We call it 'war craft,'" Moss's father said.

"Uh . . . yes . . . well, is there, say . . . umm . . . weather craft or, uh —" I desperately tried to think of another kind of craft but couldn't. "Oh well, never mind," I said as if it meant nothing to me. But it did mean something. I just couldn't quite explain it yet.

I changed the subject. "Did Kielian snakes help with those barracks?"

"You bet," Rolf replied. "Trees are scarce here, and there aren't a lot of hollows. So it's either the cliffs or ground nests, the kind that Burrowing Owls have a talent for making."

The sky was clear and the moon was rising now like a silver slit in the indigo night.

"What's Orf like, Rolf?" Moss asked.

"You have to meet him to understand him," the Elf Owl replied cryptically.

The far side of Dark Fowl buzzed with life. Owls swooped in from the front, some wounded, others puffed up with excitement over their latest feats. We passed one of the few trees on the island, a shaggy spruce with long branches thickly fringed with needles. It was an exceptionally tall tree and it seemed to shake with the loud din of owls — hooting, singing, madly talking.

"Glaux-cursed Eagle Owl tried to take me down with a fizblister! Then his buddy, a Great Gray, came in on my port side with a hook and thorn, then another with a hot blade. But the wind shifted and I was able to slide just beneath them." The owl dragged a talon across the branch on which he perched. "You see the enemy line was here." I heard a twig breaking. "Put that twig there, will ya, Igor? Ayuh, that's it."

"Rolf, what's going on there?" I asked.

"It's a grog tree. Might as well call it the 'brag tree.' It's where soldiers gather when they come back from the front. Tell their tales of valor and glory." There was a disparaging tone in his voice.

"What's wrong with that?" I asked.

Arne turned to me. "Young'un, war's not glorious and there's no courage without fear. But they come here, load up on the bingle juice, and begin to tell their tales."

Suddenly, I heard a cry from above.

"Rask!" Tantya Hanja swooped down from one of the higher branches of the tree. "Don't tell me this chick is ready to be a cadet?" I wilfed when I heard the word "chick." How could she? This was so embarrassing.

"Not yet. Not yet, Hanja, just on his first fledgling flight."

"What! And you didn't contact me? This is an occasion. It calls for a song!" She paused and caught sight of Moss. "And you're the neighbor. Of course, I met your broody. A dear thing she is. Oh, my goodness. How fast you grow. Not a trace of down and all fledged out. Turn around, let me see your tail feathers. Are they fanning yet?"

Of course they're fanning, you idiot. How could we rudder for banking turns if they didn't fan? I wanted to say. The moon had fattened and light spilled down through the spreading limbs of the tree, illuminating Hanja. Flaring above her head like a sunbolt was the bronze feather of a H'rathghar grackle. Most grackles are black with glossy iridescent plumage, but the H'rathghar grackle is distinguished by a single bronze tail feather that is buried amid the black ones and only displayed when ruddering in flight. Tantya Hanja must have found it up on the glacier. Suddenly, a completely inebriated Burrowing Owl staggered up. His eyes were soft with the witless light of a drunk.

"Ah, Hanja, you're so gosh-darned purty with that grackle feather. How about a little snuggle in the wuggle?"

"Beat it, you cretin," she yelled at him, and shoved him aside, then lofted herself into the air and began hooting in a low voice.

Come, gather around, owls,
I'll tell you a tale.
It's a story you know
Perhaps all too well.
Hatched in a war
With no end in sight
Two young'uns fledged
For their very first flight.
To be a warrior, is that
What Glaux intended?
To fight to the death
In a war never ended?

Come soldiers and teachers,
Heed my call.
Lay down your weapons
And try to recall
The nights that were peaceful,
The hollows so snug.
But this war is forever raging
To the bitter end must we always fight?

Think twice of your own,
Your very first flight.
Will the first be the last and the last be the first?
Is this how our world
Shall finally be cursed?

A hush fell over the tree and then I heard my father utter a curse. "Hanja, get out of here with your frinkin' notions of peace!"

I was mortified by my tantya Hanja's song. The ideas were bad enough, but Mum had lost her eye for the war. Moss's mum's talon had been freakishly mutilated.

"I'm sorry — I'm sorry!" I murmured to Moss.

"Don't worry. Everyone knows that gadfeathers are just silly old things."

"Come along, lads," Moss's father said gruffly.

As we flew on to Orf's forge, the clangs of a hammer striking metal fell through the darkness like metallic sleet. In the scant interval between strikes, another sound seeped through the night, a low granular scraping. The clouds scudded off the moon and we found ourselves on the brink of a shallow pit — the source of the scraping noises. The fangs of two dozen or more Kielian snakes blazed like shards split from a full-shine moon.

"The honing pit," my father said.

"What?"

"Remember I told you how the forged weapons are honed to their final keenness by the Kielian snakes? It's just a short distance from here to Orf's forge, and he recruits the best snakes, so most of the smiths bring their swords, battle claws, and daggers here."

"Gragg." An elderly snake was addressing a younger Kielian, a deeply glistening cobalt-colored snake. The elderly snake was azure and spotted. "You need to brace that blade better between the clamping rocks so your fangs can get the correct angle on the blade. Makes all the difference."

Gragg grunted unpleasantly.

The older snake caught sight of us.

"Ah, Rask! Arne! Good to see you. Hear you had some action over on the Ice Dagger."

"A bit, yes. Orf's in, I take it?" my father asked.

"Oh, yes. I better get back to the pit." The older snake lowered his voice. "Some of these new young snakes are awfully lazy." He slid his eyes toward the cobalt one he had addressed as Gragg.

In two or three wing beats we were at the forge, but it was several minutes before Orf noticed us.

"Never interrupt a smith at his forge," Da whispered. "Dangerous. We just wait patiently. Eventually, he'll notice we're here."

Finally, the owl set down his hammer and tongs.

"Now, when you use that Persuader in combination with a dagger, it's my sense that it's best if you keep the dagger in your starboard talon and the Persuader in your port one. Then you can advance using a beat/parry sequence with the Persuader and a compound riposte with your dagger."

It was as if Orf had simply picked up a conversation with my da at a point where they had left off. "Beat/parry," "compound riposte" — these were phrases I had never before heard. But I was soon to see them in action, because Orf reached for a needle-like sliver of metal that I presumed was the Persuader, and then a dagger still hot from the fires. He lofted himself into the air with a weapon in each talon and began to zigzag across the night. The blades flashed as he battled an invisible opponent. Darting up and down, he thrust and sliced at the air. There was nothing frantic about the action; it was controlled, but so fast! The whistle of the tempered edges sizzled in the night as he rolled onto his back and jabbed at the moon.

He was a spectacular flier. Neither Moss nor I had ever seen such a display of wings and blades. He alighted on a rock a short distance from the fires of his forge, then looked at Moss and me as if seeing us for the very first time.

"Your lads?" he asked, nodding toward our fathers.

"That they are," Arne replied. "My son, Moss, and that young fellow is Lyze."

With just a brief nod, nothing more, Orf acknowledged our presence.

"I take it there was an incident at the Ice Dagger? Friedl stopped by. Sorry about Piet. He was a good scrapper and would have made a fine harvester."

"They want our ice," Arne said.

Orf turned around and reached for something with his talons. When he swiveled his head back, his face looked very odd.

"Goggles," my father explained. Moss and I blinked. We had never seen anything like this before — two blue transparent disks worn over Orf's eyes.

"They're mostly worn by small owls, like Pygmies and Elf Owls, who work with ice splinters in very close combat," Arne said.

"Wish I could get you big fellows to use them," Orf said, and peeled them off with a talon. "And don't tell me the weight is too much. If a Pygmy can fly with them, so can you. Safety measure." I saw my da's head droop. He was, I knew, thinking of my mum's lost eye, rolling around someplace in the Everwinter Sea.

"When will these young'uns be coming on as cadets?" Orf asked. Moss and I both swiveled our heads toward our fathers.

"Come the soffen issen,"[11] Da replied.

Spring! I thought. It was so far off.

"Well, let me get them some liffen claws so they can practice."

"Liffen claws!" Moss and I both lofted up a short distance at this news. Light claws or training claws were terribly exciting. If we could master flying well with them, we might be able to get into one of the advanced classes when we became cadets at the Academy.

"That's very kind of you, Orf," Moss's father replied.

The blacksmith disappeared into his ground lodge and came back with a large botkin filled with training battle claws. It took him no time to fit out Moss with a set of gizzard-rippers. It was a particular style that was very good for tearing through belly flesh and feathers to get at a gizzard. I couldn't help but

------

11   The Northern Kingdoms have different names for the seasons from the Southern Kingdoms. In the Southern Kingdoms, the seasons are named after the hues of the milkberries that grow on the vines of the Great Ga'Hoole Tree. There is the White Rain, which is winter, followed by the Silver Rain for spring. Then summer is the Golden Rain, and autumn, the Copper-Rose Rain. In the Northern Kingdoms, the seasons' names are based on the condition of snow and ice. Soffen issen or "soft ice" is spring. Ny schnee is summer and literally means "no snow." Autumn is liffen schmoo, or "light frost," and winter is brikta schnee or "deep snow." During winter, however, there are several more ways to describe snow depending on the kind it is and when it falls. Siypah schnee is snow that falls at dawn. Krepla schnee is snow that falls very fast and is blinding.

think if I had those on the Ice Dagger, I could have killed that Barn Owl all by myself. The training claws were blunt tipped, of course. Orf finally found me a more general type of battle claws. We learned how to put them on properly and take them off. It was awkward trying to fasten them.

"You practice, lads. You have to be able to claw up within seconds," Orf said.

Flying with the battle claws was not as difficult as I had imagined. Once you got used to the weight, it was fairly simple, although my wings grew tired more quickly. But Moss and I were determined to practice every night.

CHAPTER 9

A Flyaway

Our parents, all four of them, had to return to the front almost immediately upon our return from Dark Fowl, for indeed it had been confirmed that the front had moved closer. Bylyric was getting bolder. It was even said that in the far north — the upper H'rath of the H'rathghar glacier — Ice Talon fighters had taken to plucking up newborn snow leopard cubs — eating babies! Bylyric had developed a taste for them!

But we were most anxious about the rumors of enemy slipgizzles in places they'd never been before. It was hard to believe that in our quiet forest of pine, oak, fir, and birch, a slipgizzle might be lurking. What could ever interest a spy here? For life was indescribably boring.

Moss and I practiced constantly, flying about with our liffen claws and picking up sticks and pretending they were real weapons. Broody Gundesfyrr was installed on the nest where Mum had been sitting on the egg. I could tell Mum was done with domestic life and was aflutter to get back to combat. I couldn't help but notice, as Mum climbed off the nest and Gundesfyrr hoisted herself up, that Mum's brood patch was tiny compared to Gundesfyrr's. The brood patch is a nearly bare spot on the belly that keeps eggs extra warm because it has a high density of blood vessels. Gundesfyrr's was twice as big as Mum's. Well, she was a professional after all, and Mum? Mum was a commando in the Ice Dagger unit.

Moss and I were big enough now that we could go out each evening at tween time and practice. We were supposed to stick close to our trees, but we never did. One evening, long after tween time, Moss and I were exploring a birch grove on the southwest side of Stormfast. We were on the cusp of the small seasons that fall between the midwinter moons and are known as lintla schnee (snow with vapor), and astrilla schnee (snow with starlight). However, on this night, these two disparate types of snow were falling at the same time. It created a peculiar effect against the white bark of the trees, almost as if the tree trunks were rippling. Above the tops of the trees, however, crisp snowflakes mingled with the starlight.

We had just settled on a branch where we could best enjoy the two snows when I looked across and saw a slight bulge on the neighboring tree trunk. At first, I thought it was a gall. Galls are abnormal growths on trees caused by mites or insects, and can eventually strangle a tree. But this particular gall seemed to be shrinking instead of growing larger. All of a sudden, I realized it was not a gall, but a wilfing Snowy Owl.

"There's an owl in that tree across the way, Moss," I whispered. "A Snowy."

"Is she clawed?" he asked.

I glanced over sharply, but her talons were bare and she appeared to be the least likely warrior in the world. She flinched with fear, and I felt sorry for her. I had the feeling she might be an orphan.

"Should we say something?" I asked Moss.

"You're asking me?"

"Well, you're a Snowy. She's your species!" I'm not sure what I was thinking. It was sort of a stupid thing to say, because it's not like there's an etiquette or guide for each species. "I feel sorry for her."

"Me too," Moss said.

"Hi," I said finally. It was barely a whisper.

"Hi there!" Moss greeted her softly.

"Me?" she answered back. Moss and I looked at each other.

"Yeah, you," Moss said. "There's no one else around."

"You sure?" she replied.

"Pretty sure," I said.

"You won't tell?" she asked.

"Tell what?"

"I — I —" she began to stammer. "I'm a flyaway."

"You mean, you have no hollow?" Moss asked. "No mum, no da?" We had heard tales of flyaways but never met one.

"Me mum died in a battle down in the Ice Talons." This Snowy had a brogue I had never heard before. Nothing like my da's brogue from the Tridents. "And me da got himself a new mate. She doesn't like me much. So I left."

"Left?" Moss said. "Just up and left?"

"Ya. She was really mean. Calls me 'Splotch.' I've had the gray scale, as you can see. Left these ugly patches."

"That's cruel," I said.

"That's Rodmilla," she replied.

"Rodmilla?" Moss said.

"Me stepmum."

"But what's your name?" Moss and I flew over to the branch where she perched.

"Thora," she answered.

"Thora! That's a beautiful name," I said. "Where are you from?"

"Oh, my accent. Yes. Firth of Canis."

"Firth of Canis!" Moss exclaimed. "I've heard of that. It's way to the north. Why are you here — so far away?"

"It's hard to explain, but . . ." She hesitated. "Me stepmother made me life insufferable." Thora clamped her eyes shut as if the very thought scorched her gizzard.

"Where will you go?"

"Maybe . . . maybe Dark Fowl."

"You mean to become a cadet," I said.

"No, a smith." She swelled up and her yellow eyes burned bright with excitement.

"A smith?" I asked. "A blacksmith?" She nodded. "But we were just there maybe a moon ago, and we didn't see a single female smith."

Thora suddenly swelled up to twice her size. "Well, it's about time!" she roared. After this sudden and completely unexpected outburst, Thora eyed our blunt-tipped battle claws.

"You know," she said. "I could make those training claws into real battle claws for you."

"You can?"

"Follow me," she said. She spread her wings and lofted off the branch. She was a lovely flier. I could tell she had a deep sense of the wind as we skimmed through the trees of the birch grove to a small, wooded glade. She began plying the cross-currents that were blowing in at odd angles and then tilted her wings and began to wheel into a steep turn. Looking down, I could see below a dim glow through the vapor snow. We alighted on a good-sized table rock. Just beneath us was a pit surrounded by large, scorched stones.

"What is it?" Moss asked.

"What does it look like?" Thora countered.

"A forge?" I replied tentatively.

"Exactly. A secret forge."

"But whose forge?"

"A Rogue smith. A Burrowing Owl's. That's why it is so beautifully excavated."

"Aren't you afraid he might come back?"

"He's dead. I found his body. It was nearly gone. Ground predators, raccoons and such. But I took the remains and burned them."

"And he left his tools?" Moss said.

"Yes, and they are beautifully made. He was a master."

"Aren't you worried someone might come back to look for him and, well, become suspicious if you're here and not the Burrowing Owl?"

"I don't think anyone knew he was here." She lowered her voice. "I think he was an arms trader to both sides."

"That's awful!" I hissed. I was astounded that someone would try to play both sides of a war. Moss and I were both silent for several seconds as we tried to grapple with this idea.

"What do you do here, Thora?" asked Moss.

"I practice. By the time I get to Dark Fowl, I am going to be the best apprentice Orf has ever seen. If he turns me down because I am a female, well, that's so pathetic I can't even bother thinking about it," she huffed. "C'mon. Want me to turn those training claws into something real?"

"Sure!" we both said.

We stayed until the darkness began to slip away and the sky turned to gray.

"Where in hagsmire have you two been?" Gilda hissed when we returned. Moss and I both blinked. We had never heard a nest-maid snake swear.

"Don't blink! I can swear. I can swear like the best of them. Do you two realize it's almost twixt time?"

Gilda began flicking her forked tongue, sniffing. This is the way snakes pick up scents. "You've been near fire, haven't you?" She narrowed her eyes, coiled up, flashed her fangs, then hissed, "Don't you dare lie to me!" She was absolutely fearsome. My gizzard seized. I really thought that she might turn her head into a hammer and smash us to smithereens.

"All right!" I said. "But you must promise not to tell Gundesfyrr — please!" Her eyes glittered. She nodded her head.

"We have to really trust you on this, Gilda," Moss said. "For in telling you, we are sort of — no, not sort of — *really* breaking a promise."

"Oh, dear," she said, suddenly contrite. "I wouldn't want you to do that." Her coil, which had been piled high, shrank suddenly. She was literally unraveling. "Oh, no, no. Trust is all we have in a civilized world. If we cannot trust each other, we have nothing."

"You really don't want to know?" I was dumbfounded.

"Don't tell me," she said in a firm voice that brooked no argument.

I tipped my head to one side to study this curious snake.

For the next several nights, Moss and I went to the secret forge to watch Thora refashion our training claws into true battle claws. Gilda always covered for us. She never asked questions, but one could see her almost savoring the scents that clung to our feathers. And indeed, there was a touch of envy in her eyes. She so clearly sought adventure beyond that of stalking the vermin in our nest.

Both Moss and I thought Thora was improving as a smith before our eyes. She had had a rather brutal way with the hammer in the beginning, but she became more adept in wielding it and delivering small, very precise strikes, the kind that make the sharp cutting edge of a blade, or in this case the edges of our battle claws. Getting rid of the blunt tips was the easy part, but honing the edges was difficult, especially considering there were no Kielian snakes around to finish them off. To achieve the sharpest edge possible, she had to heat and reheat the claws numerous times. It was fascinating to watch the claws go through the shifting spectrum of color. In the beginning, the metal was cool gray, but as it heated, it became a dark red, then an almost translucent orange, and finally yellow, the color indicating the greatest heat.[12] At certain points, the claws were withdrawn from the fire and hammered. Then, once again, Thora would put them back into the flames. The reason she had been in the birch grove the night we met her was to collect the papery bark of the trees, as it was excellent kindling.

We loved our visits to the secret forge. The memory of those is incised in my mind's eye. The forge was in the center of a circle of fir trees, and we would perch on scattered rocks or a large stump, upwind of Thora's fires. As the night darkened, the flames grew brighter and Thora's hammer struck the anvil faster and faster as our training claws became instruments of death. Sparks swirled up, enveloping Thora in a cocoon of radiance. Above, the crowns of the fir trees sifted the light of a nearly full moon.

On the fifth night, the claws were finally finished.

"Now, you two listen to me," Thora said, and suddenly she seemed much older than her years. "Use these well. Don't be stupid. And here's something else." She reached for a botkin.

"What's that?" I asked, peering into the small bucket that collier owls used to collect coal.

---

12 Years later while at the Great Ga'Hoole Tree, I spent many hours in the forge of the tree's legendary blacksmith, Bubo, who had trained with Orf. My observations are collected in a small volume, *The Spectrum of the Forge: Color Theory and Analysis*.

"Caps," she replied.

"What for?" But as soon as Moss asked the question, it dawned on us. Our fathers had left us with blunt-tipped training claws, not fighting ones, not razor-sharp battle claws. Any grown-up who saw these would be furious. We were considered too young to wield such deadly weapons.

"Thora, we don't know how to thank you," I said.

She hesitated a moment before replying. "I know how," she said, and cast her eyes down shyly. "You can come back. Come back and visit me."

"Of course!" we both said.

"I was afraid that when I finished your claws, you'd stop coming. That's why it took me so long. I'm — I'm so alone here."

"Come back with us," I said. "To my hollow."

"Or mine," Moss chimed in.

"No. No, I can't. I have to stay at this secret forge." She cast her eyes toward the dying flames. "I have to practice."

So we did come back, from the time of the lintla schnee through the full glorious nights of the astrilla schnee and then into the time of the krepla schnee, the blinding snow.

CHAPTER 10

Lysa!

Toward the end of the blinding snow, we returned from visiting Thora one evening to find Gundesfyrr quite excited. She was almost bouncing up and down on the nest.

"It's rocking. It's rocking!" she exclaimed. "The egg is rocking!"

I was suddenly very frightened. "Oh! Is that bad? What does it mean?"

"It's not bad at all. It means the chick is about to hatch."

"Really?" I was overwhelmed with excitement. Until now, that egg had been the most boring thing in the world. "Get off. Let me see!" I shouted. Gundesfyrr lifted one leg delicately and tipped sideways, supporting herself on her starboard wing so I could have a peek beneath the bald spot on her belly. The egg was jiggling just the tiniest bit and, every once in a while, it acutally rocked.

We waited through the night, me driving Gundesfyrr mad with my questions. Every two seconds, I asked if the egg was rocking again; I was hopping from one foot to the other.

"Quit jumping around so much," Gundesfyrr scolded.

"I'm — I'm not jumping. I am inspiring her . . . him, whoever!"

I even made up a little song to entice the chick to come out.

> *Jump, jump!*
> *Bump, bump!*
> *Wouldn't it be somethin'*
> *If you just started thumpin'.*
> *A little crack is all you need,*
> *No wider than a tiny seed.*
> *It's much more fun outside*
> *Than in.*
> *Now crack that egg,*
> *Let the party begin!*

"Oh, great Glaux!" Gundesfyrr's large yellow eyes opened very wide. "I think you have inspired something. I feel the egg tooth. Time to get off."

Gundesfyrr began raising herself off the nest very slowly, very gracefully, as if she were about to softly take flight. When she was finally off, she gave a little flip of her head, inviting me to step up to the nest. "No loud noises," she whispered. "We want the chick to be able to concentrate. This is the hardest work it has ever had to do."

"What work?" I asked.

"The egg tooth. Don't you see it poking through?"

I peered. "That . . . that . . . that little thing?" It was a glistening bead no bigger than a dewdrop, peeking up from inside the egg. But it was attached to something that was alive. It was moving. "Is it really a tooth?"

"They call it that, but no. It is just a little pointy bump on the top of the chick's beak. It's only used for this one single purpose — to crack the egg — and will drop off a few days after the chick hatches."

I gasped.

"Don't worry," Gundesfyrr said. "I'll find it. I always do. Broodies are good at finding egg teeth."

"Did you find mine?"

"Of course I did. Didn't I say I always found them?"

"Is this chick ever going to get out?" I muttered.

"It's taking a rest right now. You must be patient. As I said, this is the hardest thing this little critter has ever had to do."

Twixt time was coming on. The light in the hollow had changed. I began to yawn; indeed I might have been half asleep when suddenly there was a crackle followed by a soft plop.

"She's here!" Gundesfyrr exclaimed.

"Was I asleep? How could you let me fall asleep?"

"What a charmer!"

I gasped. She was, well, frankly, sort of a disaster.

"Is she breathing?" I asked.

"Of course she is. Aren't you, sweetie?" Gundesfyrr tweeted to what I can only describe as a wet blob. "Come close, dear, take a look at your new sister."

I was frightened. I took one tiny step. My gizzard was fluttering like my plummels in a crosswind. Now let me tell you something. The closer I came to the nest, the more nervous I got. Something deeper was stirring — a realization. And this was it: A newly hatched chick is not a thing of beauty. But it is a thing of love. My sister, Lysa, was pure love.

"Oh . . . oh . . ." I began to sputter. My gizzard had never been so stirred. I could not utter the words to express my joy, my admiration, my passion for this little, wet creature still streaked in the threads of blood from the yolk. She was covered with strange little swirls of wet fuzz, her bare flesh showed through, and her eyes were sealed shut and looked like outsized bumps on her face.

Gundesfyrr gave a mighty belch and out came some partially digested vole.

"Been saving that one for you, darling. Your first meal."

"Is that what she eats? Throw up?"

"It's easy on their tummies. She eats that along with the first slime from her eggshell. Chicks can't really make pellets yet."

I opened my beak and tried to belch but only a little squeak issued forth. "Oh, dear, I don't think I have any of that mouse left. It's already packed in a pellet for yarping."

"Next time, just save some. Don't let it go to your gizzard too fast."

"You can do that?"

"Oh, yes, if you concentrate." I must have looked very close to despair, for Gundesfyrr extended a wing and stroked me. "Don't worry. There'll be many more chances. This is what she'll eat until her first insect."

I had a battery of questions. My beak couldn't keep up with my brain. "When will her eyes open?"

"Not for a while. Ten nights or more. And let's hope at night."

"Why?"

"Oh, daylight is much too harsh, and it's bad luck to open your eyes in the daylight. Nighttime is owl time."

That was all I needed to hear. I became insanely diligent watching over little Lysa. I was absolutely obsessed with the idea that she should not open her eyes in the daytime. I like to think I am a rational bird, but all reason went out the hollow when I heard this. Of course, I had no idea what I would do if she did open her eyes during daylight. Clamp my talons over them and maybe injure her by accident?

Moss's siblings hatched out soon after Lysa. All three were little females, much to his disappointment. "I thought I would get at least one male out of the clutch," he grumbled.

"Well, now Lysa can have three little girl friends. It will be

nice for them. They'll entertain each other and we can go off."
I nodded in the direction of the secret forge. What with all this
hatching, it had been a while since we had visited Thora and
we had promised to come back. I really didn't want to leave
until Lysa opened her eyes. I wanted to be the first face she saw.
Maybe it was selfish. Maybe I had delusions of importance. But
I was, in fact, her only blood relative around. Even though
Gundesfyrr was her broody and still brooding her, for a naked
little chick has nothing to protect it from the cold and we were
getting the first of the dryflifa schnee, the kind of snow that
clings to feathers. With it came very cold temperatures and
some snurlish winds.

Several nights after Lysa hatched, I had just yarped some
white-footed mouse for her when I noticed a flitter beneath the
skin that covered her eyes.

"Gundesfyrr, look! I think her eyes are . . . are . . ."

First one eye slit opened and then two or three seconds
later — it seemed like forever — the other one opened and a
tiny voice muttered a single word.

"Again?"

"She can talk!"

"Of course she can." Gilda slithered over. "She's heard all of
us talking for the last, what has it been? Nine nights?"

"Again?" Lysa said again.

"Again what?" I asked.

"Mouseth," she sighed. When she spoke she had a slight lisp. It was the cutest thing ever. "Tired of mouseth. No vole?" She paused. "Pleath, Lyze."

My heart seized, my gizzard lurched when I heard her speak my name.

"You know my name?"

"Yeth. You my big brother." I blinked but the tears wouldn't stop.

"Don't cry," Lysa chirped. "I love you. Eyes not for crying." She opened her own so wide and began swiveling her head around like an old pro. "You Gilda?" she said, then flipped her head upside down and backward. "And you my broody, Gundie!" She took a big breath. "I LOVE LOVE LOVE all you!"

Lysa began to grow in leaps and bounds. She was the fluffiest fuzzball ever and each day there was a new achievement. She had her First Insect ceremony, then First Meat. I could hardly tear myself away from her to go visit Thora, but we did sneak off occasionally.

"I understand about little sisters." Thora paused and seemed to gulp. We thought she was about to say something, but she turned back to her work. "You know, they grow very quickly. You should make a chart."

"A chart?"

"Yes. Go over to my kindling pile and each of you take a big piece of birch bark and then fetch yourself a nice charred piece of wood and you'll have a marker."

"Now what?" Moss asked.

"Start marking down what your sisters do!"

"You mean their sky marks?" I asked. For that is the word we used for significant events in a growing owlet's life, even before they can fly.

"Yes. You know, when they hatch, when they eat, followed by their first yarped pellet."

It was a wonderful idea, and Moss and I both started the charts for our sisters.

"Can I put three on one chart?" Moss asked.

"I wouldn't if I were you," Thora advised. "They each deserve their own sky marks chart."

I looked at Thora. She was an uncommonly intelligent owl and not that much older than we were, but somehow vastly more mature.

CHAPTER 11

A Visit from Tantya Hanja

That day, I returned to the hollow close to twixt time, and Lysa woke up.

"Lyze, that you?"

"Of course. Why are you awake?"

"I've got this funny feeling in my tummy."

"You do?"

"Yes, ever since my First Meat last night."

"You do!" I was terribly excited. I had arrived just in time with my chart. "Don't panic, Lysa. Stay calm."

"I am calm."

"This is nothing to worry about." I took a big breath. "You are about to yarp your first pellet."

"I thought it might be something like that. I think I'm budging, too. I just didn't want to wake up Gundie."

"We'll help you, dear," Gilda said.

"Now here's what we do," I said. "I'm going to lead you to the very edge of the hollow. And you have to lean out and open your mouth very wide."

Lysa followed me to the portal and I helped her to the ledge just outside.

"Oh, my, it's so beautiful! The snow looks pink."

"It's dawn snow, siypah schnee."

"This is so exciting. I've never been up this late. I've never seen the day!" She paused. "I've never seen the night for that matter. I've just heard about stars and the moon. Look, there's one star left over from the night!"

"That's the Light Bringer, the morning star. The one that climbs into the dawn before the sun rises."

"It's lovely. I never thought there would be lovely things that were part of the day. I thought it was only the night that hatched beautiful treasures like stars and moonlight."

"You won't be able to see the Light Bringer for long. Not after the sun rises. But now you must concentrate on that pellet. How's it coming?"

"Oh, that!" she replied dismissively.

"Not 'oh, that!' This is important. We'll mark it on your chart. Come on now. This is your chance to show how grown up you are. Open your beak really wide," I urged her.

Lysa opened her beak as wide as she could.

"Now you're ready to yarp," I said. "Make a little hiccup. That's it . . . that's it. Go for it! It's coming. I can hear it rumbling."

Something flew out of her mouth.

"You did it!" I exclaimed.

"Where'd it go?"

"Down there. A nice plump pellet. When you start to eat the meat on bones with fur, all your pellets will even be bigger."

"Oh, my Glaux, I might not be up to a really big pellet."

"Of course you will."

Lysa looked down, trying to spot where the pellet had landed.

"You want me to fetch it? We'll show Gundesfyrr when she wakes up."

"What a lovely idea!" Gilda said. "I'll go down and get it."

I heard a flapping sound in the distance. *That's rather loud,* I thought. A dread seeped through my gizzard. Lysa must have picked up on it.

"What is it, Lyze?" she asked.

"What is it?" a familiar voice hooted like a slightly distorted echo.

Oh, Glaux! It was Tantya Hanja. I saw Gilda freeze in her tracks.

Go away! I wanted to schreech. But she was our aunt.

"Oh, my goodness. What an adorable little owlet," Hanja said.

"I just yarped my first pellet!" Lysa said. She tucked her wings behind her and swung her tail back and forth a bit, she was so proud.

"Oh, melt my gizzard!" cooed Tantya Hanja.

Gilda had climbed back up the tree with the pellet coiled in her tail.

"Do come in," she said politely, then gave me a rather sharp nudge with her head as if scolding me for forgetting my manners.

"Yes, do come in," I repeated. "So — so . . . happy to see you," I lied.

"Any voles? White-footed mice?" she asked as we entered the hollow. "I love the voles from this woods. They're very sweet." Have I mentioned that Tantya Hanja was a bit of a mooch? She always traveled with a botkin and happily received any gifts that owls bestowed on her. And they bestowed many in an effort to get rid of her quickly.

"No white-footed mice, but I'd be happy to get you some," I said quickly.

Usually, when I went out hunting, I went bare-taloned. But I knew Tantya Hanja was an incredibly nosy old Screech. Always poking about the hollow under the guise of nest-keeping, as she had just begun to do.

"Oh, Gilda, I think you missed some inchworms in that corner," she called.

I didn't want her poking around my battle claws and discovering the caps that disguised the sharp tips. So I put them on.

"Your training claws, Lyze! How handsome. You wear them for white mice? Hardly seems worth the effort."

"I need all the practice I can get."

"You'll make a wonderful cadet. When do you go to the Academy?"

Not soon enough, I wanted to say. "Soffen issen," I replied.

"Spring? Well, that's not too far off. This little one might be flying by then."

I hoped so. I couldn't wait until Lysa could fly. In a very few weeks when the snow wasn't too heavy in the trees, I planned to start her on branching.

CHAPTER 12

The Molt of a Warrior

"So," Moss said, flying out of his hollow, "I see your tantya Hanja has arrived." I made a scathing sound deep in my throat. "You're not alone," Moss said. "Her showing up is enough to put the entire forest on edge."

"Shhh," I said as I picked up the first heartbeats of what I was certain was a white-footed mouse. Moss tilted his head to scoop up the tiny footfalls.

"We've got competition!" he said.

"What?"

"A Snowy. I know the wing beats."

Suddenly, out of the thickly falling snow, hurled a sooty sphere with wings. "Thora!"

"They're coming! They're coming. It's an attack!"

"Who? What?"

"Ice Talon commandos with fire claws."

Fire claws! No decent owl fought with fire claws. They were grosnik, forbidden, dirty weapons.[13]

---

13 Fire claws were considered not just dirty but the most dangerous of all weapons. With them, an owl can fight at close range while actually

Thora was armed to the beak. She had battle claws, a scimitar in one talon and a billy hook in the other. "They stole embers from my forge to load their claws. They're coming!"

Moss and I both hooted the alarm calls of our species. The Snowy alarm is like a hot needle piercing the air while my own is a hollow warble in a higher frequency. Within seconds, the small forest at our end of Stormfast Island was shrieking. Then, like fiends from hagsmire, the enemy swooped down on us.

Their faces were emblazoned with the double red crescents, the sign of their so-called sacred force. "Bhachtyr Bylyric!" they screeched as they raised the tips of their glowing fire claws in the name of Bylyric. Their battle cry did not frighten me, but it did sicken me. I felt my gizzard boil. I was ready to fight — to fight as savagely as any creature on Earth. It was as if I had instantly molted into a new bird, almost unrecognizable to myself. How my heart did pound. I felt nothing except rage, cool rage that left my brain clear. I was able to make a quick assessment of the battlefield: where they were and what they were fighting with.

Some were armed with scimitars, others with hot blades, hooks, thorns, and all manner of weapons including ice

---

ripping and burning an opponent. However, they were not only injurious to the enemy, but over time they disfigure an owl's talons. Orf would not permit fire claws to be made on Dark Fowl, and many blacksmiths refused to make them.

blades. Somehow their ice looked slightly different from the shards we saw harvested at the Ice Dagger. Elfstrom, the large Snowy from a neighboring tree, was back from the front and leaped into the air to engage a Burrowing Owl.

Burrowing Owls are not the best fliers. Their long, featherless legs are made for digging, and this one appeared to be digging at the air as if it were soil. In the process, he dropped his ice splinter. I swooped down and retrieved it. It was light and didn't throw me off balance at all. I had seen owls practicing with the splinters on Dark Fowl and knew you could hurl an ice splinter or use it for talon-to-talon combat. I decided to hurl this one. As soon as I saw a space between Elfstrom and the Burrowing Owl open up, I raised my talon, aimed for the owl's chest, and flung it. A spurt of blood smeared the night. The owl plummeted toward the ground.

"On your tail, Lyze!"

I smelled singed feathers. My feathers! A Barred Owl with fire claws had attacked me from the rear. I operated on pure instinct and began backwinging, then flipped myself tailfirst into a small snowdrift and smothered the smoldering sparks. It was a contour, or covering feather, that had caught fire, and luckily not one of my filos.[14]

---

14 Filoplumes are very fine feathers beneath the covering feathers with a nearly invisible shaft. They are exceedingly sensitive to pressure and vibrations. These filos have the extraordinary ability to sense the location of the other feathers when an owl is in flight, so that subtle wing adjustments can be made as necessary.

"Brilliant!" a familiar voice called from above. I looked up. I was under my hollow's tree and directly above me, a creature was swinging something that looked like a scaled flail. It was Gilda. She had transformed her head into a weapon and was swinging it at Ice Talon owls.

But there was not time to marvel. I saw Thora and Moss together fending off a threesome of Barn Owls. There was a dead Great Gray nearby on the ground, his fire claws hissing softly in the snow as the coals in their tips expired. Beside him lay an ice scimitar four times the size of the splinter I'd hurled. I seized it with both my claws, then transferred it to my port talon. I realized immediately that I would have to compensate for its weight by stroking harder with my starboard wing, but I flew toward the rear of the three Barn Owls as fast as I could. They were flying in a tight formation, their wings almost touching, and they didn't see me. But Moss and Thora saw it all. I lifted the scimitar and came down hard with it in the tight spaces between two of the owls. They screeched, and two tawny wings fell to the ground, their owners plummeting after. The third owl turned and opened his eyes wide with fear, but before he could maneuver, Thora and Moss were on him. They ripped open his back and tore off his tail.

Moss's eyes glazed over with a look of absolute horror. "Your tree! Your tree!" he shrieked. There was a loud cracking sound and then a sweet smell. The tree burst into flame, fire leaping toward the sky and scorching the night.

"Lysa!" I shrieked, and flew straight toward the fiery hollow. The sound of owls battling receded behind me. I had only one thought in my mind: Save my sister! The tree hissed and spat as boiling sap escaped from the trunk and branches. A dark mouth seemed to widen before me. It was the hollow, spewing black smoke. I flew in but could not breathe. I instinctively backed out. There simply was not enough air. But I was determined to try again. I'd find another way. I'd tear a hole in the trunk on the backside if I had to. The awful odor of seared feathers mixed now with the sweetness of the sap. I flew through the branches of the pine desperate to find a back way into my family's hollow, choking and shreeing in horror. Then I felt something raking me from the tree. There was the cool draft of air in my lungs. And that was the last I remembered.

"He's coming around," I heard someone whisper. I could still smell that sickeningly sweet odor of boiling sap from the burning tree. My eyes blinked open. Elfstrom was bending over me, his yellow eyes bright and anxious in a white face now black with soot. Thora's and Moss's faces were also darkened from the ashes and smoke. I tried to speak but began coughing and couldn't get a word out.

"Don't try to talk." Elfstrom patted me with his wing as gently as possible for he still wore his battle claws. I shut my eyes and, concentrating as hard as I could, tried not to cough.

Finally, I gasped, "Lysa!" I saw Elfstrom glance nervously at Moss. Gilda slithered up to me. Her head had resumed its normal contours, and tears rolled out of both her eyes. "She's gone, Lyze."

"They snatched her!"

"No, dear." She shook her head wearily. "She's dead."

A revulsion pulsed through me. My gizzard quaked. *Dead? Lysa can't . . . can't be dead. She just budged. I was going to teach her to fly. . . .* It was all so wrong.

"Gundesfyrr, too," Gilda said. "It was the smoke. They suffocated in the hollow and you nearly did, too."

Moss began to speak. "Gilda got to you and dragged you out."

"I went back in for Lysa. I found her, but it was too late."

"You found her?"

"And Gundesfyrr." She nodded slightly to one side. I twisted my head. There they lay. Next to Gundesfyrr's rather large body, Lysa was nothing more than a little dark lump in the snow. All her lovely tawny feathers that had just begun to budge were an awful sooty color. And Gundesfyrr had been a handsome Spotted Owl, but not one of her spots showed through the black. Her sister, Prytlah, stood over her, weeping. But it was the sight of Tantya Hanja that made me shut my eyes. She had nary a scorched feather, not a trace of ash in her plumage. How had she escaped while the rest . . . I didn't finish the thought. She was hunched over Lysa's tiny body, weeping clamorously. I couldn't look. I had to try and remember Lysa's tawny feathers and the gray ones, and the flecks of white feathers that would have soon appeared over her eyes. *Mum was wrong*, I thought. *A pine tree isn't the safest tree in the forest. It was the sap that caused it to ignite.*

And Lysa? Lysa had passed over that border between Earth and glaumora. The echoes of her churring voice when she laughed at my pranks, the merry glint in her eyes when she heard me talk of flight — all these I would keep precious and bright. I would polish them as a smith polishes his metalwork to keep the gleam. She was not here on Earth with me, but she was somewhere. . . . *Somewhere*, I thought.

The rage that had overtaken my gizzard and my heart was still inside me. The savage bird within had been unrecognizable to me at first, but he was beginning to feel quite familiar. I slipped into his plumage as easily as during a spring molt. For the season of the soldier had arrived, and I was ready to tap that boiling rage again.

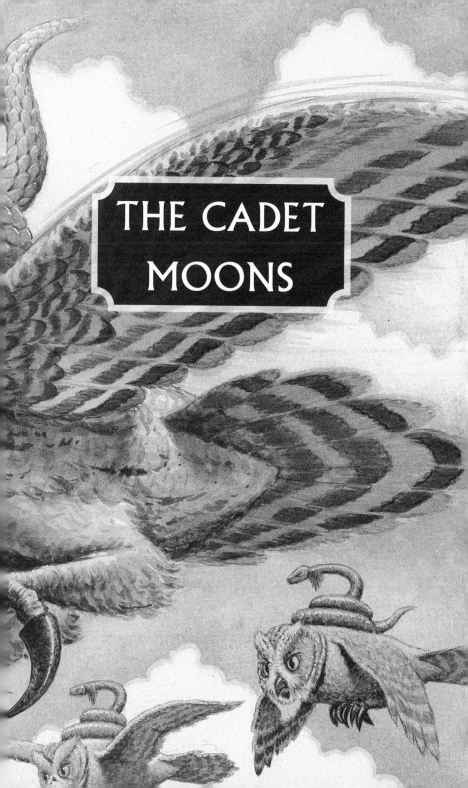

THE CADET
MOONS

CHAPTER 13

The Academy

Moss's sisters had all survived. Their hollow was not in a pine tree, which had turned out to be a veritable firetrap. My parents returned soon after the tragic attack. They had seen a lot, but never anything quite like this, never an attack on broodies and children. My mother was stunned. She kept hopping around in the charred debris of the tree, as if she were searching for some tiny remnant — a toy, perhaps even an old yarped pellet of Lysa's — of her youngest chick. My father followed her, and every now and then would pat her with his wing tip and try to murmur soothing words. But there was nothing he could say. The war had changed in a way that no one had ever anticipated. No longer did warrior meet warrior on a neutral field. Bylyric had come to our peaceful forest and savaged it.

The battle in our forest had been won by what my da called a "few good owls." And he included me in that small coterie. Moss and Thora and I had distinguished ourselves. After all, we were very young owls and had not as yet experienced any kind of combat on this scale, nor had we any kind of combat training. My parents' devastation at the loss of their first daughter was eased by their pride in me. "A real soldier, this one!" my da would boom. And my mum's yellow eye would glitter fiercely. "A commando if I ever saw one," she proclaimed.

Moss, Thora, and I flew to Dark Fowl soon after the attack. We realized our childhood was finished. I had the feeling that Thora's had been finished long before. The news of the attack had reverberated throughout the Kielian League and nowhere was it more evident than on Dark Fowl. The island bustled with activity. The smiths did not sleep. Their fires burned both day and night. The honing pits had added snakes, who worked in shifts through the days and nights.

The Military Academy on Dark Fowl gave us no time to grieve. There was so much to learn, and we were busy constantly. With the attack on Stormfast, the war had escalated and we were only the first of many attacks on civilian settlements to come.

It was not easy for a young owl to arrive for training with a bit of a history behind him. At least, that's the way it was with the three of us — Moss, Thora, and myself. Everyone had heard about the attack on Stormfast. Expectations were running high for us, uncomfortably high. It was especially tough for Thora, who really had no desire to train as a cadet. She wanted to learn smithing and apprentice Orf. She would settle for an apprenticeship with no other smiths. There had never been a female smith in the history of the Northern Kingdoms; it was not a promising situation. I cringed when she asked one of our instructors once if she might take some training to work at a forge.

"A forge!" the Barn Owl, who was a female, screeched. "Are you yoickers? Females are not smith material, not at all, never ever!" And it was a female squawking at poor Thora! It was shocking to me how rigid the instructors and officers of the Kielian League were. Shocking and disheartening, for none of them seemed to have much imagination. They never entertained the idea that there might be other ways to do things.

The elite commando units were very specialized in the types of raids they implemented and the kinds of weapons they used. I wanted to do it all — sabotage, surveillance, reconnaissance. I was very interested in military strategy in general. Serving in a commando unit, no matter how elite, seemed limiting to me. But cadets couldn't pick and choose what they wanted to do or what they felt their strengths were. There was a rigid curriculum and any picking and choosing was done by the regimental commander of the Academy. That was a Barred

Owl named Optimus Strix Varia.[15] He was a stern, old owl and, although he was missing three of his four talons on his port foot, he was skillful with fizgigs and fizblisters. These spiked iron spheres on the end of lightweight chains were among the most challenging of weapons to manipulate. Inside the fizblisters were hot coals that made them even more difficult, for if the owl wielding the weapon made the slightest mistake, he could ignite his own feathers. But the fizblisters could be lethal. An attacking owl could swoop into an enemy formation and scatter it with one twirl of the weapon. There was a release mechanism on the chain that had to be operated with great precision, and experts with fizblisters could hurl them great distances. Timing was everything!

Moss, Thora, and I settled into our barracks in the outcropping of lithite rocks and began to make friends with our fellow cadets. The most memorable were Blix, a tiny Northern Sawwhet, and Loki, a Great Gray. They had known each other

---

15   It was the custom in the Northern Kingdoms for commanders in the military to be called by not simply their given names but the formal nomenclature of their species. Hence, "Strix Varia," which is the species name for a Barred Owl. My own father was known as General Raskin Megascops Trichopsis. However, cadets are addressed by their given names followed by just the first part of their species name. Therefore, I would be known as "Cadet Lyze Megascops."

since they were fledglings and made quite a pair, as Blix didn't even come up to Loki's knees. But they were fast friends. When I first met them, I could not help but notice that Loki's wing tips were a bit tattered, as if he had bashed them up somehow. I remember saying, "Looks like you have already seen some combat!" The two friends exchanged almost guilty glances.

"Oh, it was nothing," Loki said quickly. "I just got a scrape on these fresh feathers."

"Oh, yes," I said. I realized it was a source of embarrassment to Loki and I dropped the subject. "That can happen."

What interested me the most about Blix and Loki was that they came from a region in the northernmost reaches of the Bitter Sea, in fact very close to Shagdah Snurl, the coldest and darkest place on Earth. But it was not the Shagdah Snurl that intrigued me. It was the place at its very center called Nacht Sted, where my mother had told me the winds were hatched.

"Have you ever seen a wind hatch?" I asked the Great Gray and the Northern Saw-whet.

"Of course!" they both said at once. "We have a celebration when the kitibits come," Blix explained.

"Skyboshing?" Thora asked.

"It's great fun. You ride the backside — the bosh — of a curl wind."

"You ride the kitibits?" I asked. I was astounded.

"Sure we do," Blix replied.

"But you're so tiny," Thora gasped.

"I won't take offense at that," the Saw-whet said, and squared her shoulders. "But actually being small makes it easier."

"I have a question," I said slowly. The serious note in my voice caught their attention.

"We've been at the Academy for three days and have been told about all sorts of classes and exercises to turn us into skillful warriors, but no one has ever mentioned anything about weather."

"What about weather?" Moss asked.

"I mean weather interpretation — analysis. Think how helpful that would be to planning battle strategies."

"Well, I don't mean to brag," Loki said. "But they say no owl flies better than owls from Shagdah Snurl." He spread his enormous wings and lofted into flight to begin a series of beautiful curling loops. When he alighted on the ground again, Blix turned to him.

"You might not mean to brag, Loki, but that was bragging!" But she said this with good cheer. One could tell that they were used to pulling each other's feathers.

"Are there any instructors, flight instructors, here at the Academy from Shagdah?"

"There used to be one, I think," Blix said thoughtfully. "But she died a long time ago."

"That brings up another question," Thora snapped. There was an edge to her voice that we hadn't heard before.

"Gotta burr in your plummels?" Moss asked.

Wrong question, I thought.

"Yes, as a matter of fact I do."

"What is it?" I asked cautiously.

"Blix mentioned a flight instructor. A she. There are several female instructors of note here, I believe. There is a colonel who commands the Frost Beaks. A Pearl-spotted Pygmy, Esa Glaucidum Perlatum. She commands the A unit of the Frost Beaks. I hope I get into A unit because B unit is headed up by Coloniel Stellan Micrathene Whitneyi, who is about as haggish as an Elf Owl ever gets. A nasty piece of work, that one."

"What's your point, Thora?" I asked as gently as possible.

"My point is this! There are several female instructors and commanders. Your own mother, Lyze, heads up the Ice Dagger unit and was an instructor here at the Academy before that. But there is not one blacksmith on the island of Dark Fowl who is female, not one Rogue smith in the entire Northern Kingdoms who is female. I have no interest in fighting, in becoming a warrior serving in some elite commando unit. But I do have a great interest in learning how to smith the weapons these units employ in battle. When I mentioned that I wanted to study smithing and serve as an apprentice to Orf, the regimental commander nearly lost his gizzard!"

"He did?" I asked.

"Yes, he did." She paused as if to remember. "I really think I almost killed him when I said that."

The others were finding this entire story rather humorous, but I began to think about it.

"I think," Thora continued reflectively, "that the Academy has a rather narrow view of things. I mean, as Blix and Loki mentioned, the best fliers come from the Shagdah Snurl but none of the flight instructors are from there. And think about the rocks that melt in the volcanoes, the flames that must make those rocks melt. What kind of coals might they produce for a smith's forge? Ice weapons from the Dagger are said to be superior to any that are harvested from the Shag, but maybe the harvesters are looking for the wrong kind of ice? It seems to me that we should be sending owls to research up there."

"My mum lost her eye to an ice splinter," I said. "But my father said it was crudely honed. They thought it was inferior ice from up around the Shag. But I'm beginning to wonder if it was inferior or if they don't know how to make a proper cold coal with those coals from the volcano up there at the Nacht Sted."

"Precisely," Thora said. "If someone knew how to use those coals properly, well, it could be very dangerous for the Kielian League."

"You know what?" Blix often began her comments this way. She was a very reflective owl.

"What?" Thora asked.

"Well," Blix said, "with your interest in coals, and Lyze's in weather, you should come up to the Shagdah Snurl for the holidays."

"Could we?" I said excitedly. I could think of nothing better. What was home for me now anyway? The charred remains of the slender pine. The memory of Lysa. As far as I knew, Mum and Da were back at the front already. They usually were in the summer months. It would be a dream come true for me to go to the place where the winds hatch. I felt it might be a place of inspiration.

This war would never end unless some new ideas were born. But who would listen to a bunch of young owls like ourselves? The more I thought about it, the more ideas I had. A delegation should be sent to Shagdah to recruit great fliers and study the winds. Smiths should be sent to the volcanoes to examine the coals. Some should be sent to the land called the Beyond to see how the colliers retrieved coals from the ember beds of the Sacred Volcanoes there. If Bylyric had turned into an Orphan Maker, and the front was coming closer every night, there wasn't much time before the Kielian League would be overrun. Already, there were rumors that our class would be fast-tracked to graduate early and head immediately out to the front.

CHAPTER 14

Ice Squires

When our intensive training period began, our first class was scheduled before tweener. They thought that cadets learn better when hungry. The classes were larger than the beginner courses, with more owls than before. Some we had not yet met, as they had been brought in from a sub-camp on a small island off Dark Fowl where they had completed their preliminary training week. I was ordered to report to the Ice Squires, commanded by a pompous old Short-eared Owl, Captain Ludvigsen Asio Flammeus. Just to give you the flavor of the old hoot, here is how he introduced himself:

"I am Captain Ludvigsen Asio Flammeus the Fifth. My father, my grandfather, great-grandfather, and great-great-grandfather all served at this Academy after distinguished careers in the Ice Squires unit, one of the oldest units in the Kielian League. As you may know, the Ice Squires fight with both hot and cold weapons. Although, not fire claws, of course. It might also interest you to know that my family's name,

Ludvigsen, is taken from an Other,[16] a certain Erich Ludvigsen Pontoppidan, who first identified our species.[17] It is a name I carry with deep pride."

"Weird," whispered a Whiskered Screech who perched beside me on the rocks where we had assembled.

I also wondered why someone would be proud to be named after an Other and began to say, "My sentiments ex —" but the words caught in my throat as I turned to her. She was the loveliest Whiskered Screech I had ever seen.

"Did you have something to say, Cadet Lyze Megascops?" the captain asked. And this, unfortunately, is where my history caught up with me.

"Nothing, sir," I replied crisply, and gave the required salute.

"Tell me, were you as vociferous in the attack on Stormfast, where you supposedly distinguished yourself?"

"No, sir, it was very hard to breathe for all the smoke."

---

16   There was a slight gasp here as the captain said this, as the Others were rarely mentioned except in conjunction with magpies who traded materials scavenged from their ruins. There were not many ruins in the Northern Kingdoms, so the concept of the Others was vague at best for many.

17   Erich Ludvigsen Pontoppidan was a Danish bishop who published the first description of a Short-eared Owl. In Latin, the word "Flammeus" means "fiery or flaming, the color of fire." These owls are a ruddy plumage. They are not, however, by nature pompous, as Captain Ludvigsen was.

"Well, why don't you inhale all your hot air now and cease speaking!" he barked.

"Sir!" It was the lovely Screech next to me. She had raised her starboard talon.

"Yes, Cadet Lillium Megascops? You have something to say?"

"Indeed, sir. It was I who initiated the conversation with Cadet Lyze Megascops."

"So you want to take the blame, I assume?"

"Yes, sir," she answered. The captain folded his wings behind his back and strutted over to us.

"Well then, Miss Cadet!" he huffed. He was about to continue, but Lillium broke in.

"Miss Cadet Lillium Megascops, sir?"

"Do you have a hearing problem?"

"No, sir. It's — it's —" she began to stammer. "It's just that I have never heard a female cadet referred to as 'Miss.'"

"And you take issue with that?"

"Well, sir . . ." She was silent for several seconds, and I thought she was going to wilf. But quite the reverse, she seemed to increase in size. "Yes! Yes, I do take issue. We are all serving here together, and there is no need to call attention to our gender."

You could have heard a feather drop. Not just any feather but the finest fringe feather, a plummel. *Great Glaux*, I thought. I had never encountered anyone like this Lillium.

"I suggest, Miss Cadet, that along with your friend here, you inhale some of your hot air as well and shut up!" The captain turned on his talons and stormed away.

She flipped her head around toward me, winked, and whispered, "I'd say we're off to a good start, Cadet Lyze Megascops!"

Oh, great Glaux, my gizzard went into a flutter. She wasn't frightened of the old hoot at all. Despite this rather rocky beginning, the practice went rather well, even though I could hardly concentrate due to my giddy condition over Lillium. We practiced with a variety of weapons, both of ice and metal. We learned the proper way to grip an ice weapon with our battle claws, both on and off. Luckily for us, the two lieutenants, both Short-eared Owls, did most of the real instruction and they were quite nice.

"Don't let the captain get you down," said Lieutenant Artemis Asio Flammeus. "He bellows about quite a bit with the new cadets. He doesn't mean much by it." I did not want to admit it but it didn't get me down one single bit. If it hadn't been for the captain, I might never had had my encounter with Lillium.

In this first training session, our instructor set up several targets with the peculiar double crescent insignia, just like the ones we had seen emblazoned on the owls' faces who had attacked us at the Ice Dagger and on Stormfast, the night my sister died. There were perhaps twenty targets altogether, but only one had crossed crescents, which we were told were the badge of Bylyric, the Orphan Maker himself. After exposure on the training field, it would not take long for this so-called "symbol of sacred force" to lose its mystique entirely and become about as sacred as a wet pellet.

Both Lillium and I did well in the training session, which seemed to aggravate the captain. Every time Lieutenant Artemis would praise us or Lieutenant Ganymede Asio Flammeus said how well we had executed a maneuver, the captain felt compelled to find a slight flaw in our performance. "Let's not get too fanciful, Cadet Lillium Megascops." Or "Cadet Lyze Megascops, you have an odd twist on the downstroke when you wield that blade. Is that a peculiarity you picked up in the skirmish on Stormfast? Or are you just trying to be creative?" He said the word "creative" as if it were something profoundly shameful.

"No, sir," I would mutter.

For our next training session, unfortunately, Lillium was put in another group. This session focused on flight formation, or FF. FF was perhaps the most challenging exercise new cadets encountered. We were all used to flying and dealing with a variety of weather conditions, but we were not used to flying in formation. It was a new discipline, used in warfare for purposes of mutual defense and the concentration of strike power. I had heard my parents talk about it, and I knew their positions in a number of different formations. But no one ever called the formations out loud. All commands were expressed nonverbally through wing signals so the flying units could operate in total silence. Therefore, our first lesson was to learn what we called the WWS, the wing waggle signals, for a variety of maneuvers. There were perhaps two dozen or more aerobatic maneuvers that had to be mastered for flying in formation and so there was a lot of code to learn.

We began with the signals for the five basic formations — the retract and roll, the vertical break, the crossover break, the flat pass, and the tail slide. It was after midnight before they actually let us take flight and practice giving the signals and performing the first couple of maneuvers.

"Oh, sorry, old fellow!" said a Great Horned Owl, Cadet Skellig Bubo, as he bumped into me. "I'm about as graceful as a puffin with its wings gone cattywampus!" I had to laugh. Cadet Skellig came from a somewhat aristocratic family that lived in a firthkin far up in the Firth of Fangs.[18] Skellig spoke

---

18 This was the same firthkin where, according to the Legends of Ga'Hoole, Queen Siv faced down her mortal enemy, Lord Arrin, who had wanted to abduct her egg, the egg of the first king of the Great Tree, good King Hoole. The owls from this region pride themselves on their ancient lineage and many claim to be able to trace their bloodlines back to Queen Siv and her mate, King H'rath, the monarchs of the Northern Kingdoms.

very properly with the cultivated accent of the owls from that firthkin, but he was not at all stuffy or grand or self-important like Captain Ludvigsen Asio Flammeus. He had a terrific sense of humor. Indeed, he was the one who came up with the nickname for the captain — Lud-Dud, which, at the time, we all thought was hysterically funny. We did not have the most sophisticated senses of humor.

Cadet Skellig seemed somewhat older than his years and was rather small. His flight skills were not promising, but he did try hard. Blix and Loki had told me that cadets from his firthkin were usually admitted to the Academy because of their distinguished ancestry. What he lacked in skills, he more than made up for with his sense of humor and good spirits. Everyone liked Cadet Skellig Bubo. He was elected as our barracks sergeant, which meant that he had to make sure we kept our personal hollows neat — there were no nest-maid snakes in the barracks. He even helped us clean if our hollows got messy. After twixt time, no one was supposed to leave the barracks but he never reported the many who snuck out to visit the grog trees. I did myself a few times. I didn't drink the highly potent bingle juice, but it was fascinating to listen to the soldiers back from the front with their combat tales. The grog tree offered an education apart from our formal training that was very valuable.

While we were doing our drills for formation flights over the training field, I caught sight of Blix and a dozen or so

Northern Saw-whets, Pygmies, and Elf Owls practicing with ice splinters. Our flight formation instructor pointed them out.

"A Frost Beak unit in training below us," he announced. Targets had been set up on the ground, and the small owls were zooming in with their launch sticks loaded with the ice splinters. Few of them were hitting their marks. "It takes a great deal of practice," our instructor, a Brown Fish Owl named Colonel Solsten Ketupa Zeylonensis, explained as we made a flat pass over the field. "The launching stick is difficult to manipulate and requires a great deal of practice. You need to find the proper grip and there's a rhythm to it."

"May I ask a question, Colonel, sir?"

"Certainly, Cadet Lyze."

"How many ice splinters does a launcher hold?"

"Good question. Just two. Then it's back to the field quartermaster. Orf is working on a launcher with a larger capacity, but of course that has to be balanced out against the very slight weight of the small owls best suited to these weapons."

"Yes, Colonel, sir," I replied. "Thank you."

I have to admit something troubled me about this explanation. It wasn't a larger launcher that was needed, but a better system for resupplying mid-flight. And if it was a question of merely larger launchers, why couldn't bigger owls be trained to fight with ice splinters? Ice splinters were very effective weapons, very deadly. Why were Pygmies, Elf, and Northern

Saw-whets the only owls who could be trained with them? I looked down at the owls below us as we made a second flat pass. Blix was doing quite well. I nearly hadn't recognized her because all of the Frost Beaks wore protective goggles ground from blue ice, as Orf had the first time I'd met him.

Our first day of training went until almost twixt time. We were starving when we got to the dining hollow. I searched for Lil and finally found her at a nest-maid table[17] — standing at a spotted azure-back Kielian who reminded me of Hoke of Hock. I hadn't thought about Hoke or Gilda since I had arrived, but now they came to mind again. They were two of the smartest snakes I had ever met and it seemed ridiculous to me that snakes were being used — I might even say misused — as dining tables. They had more to contribute. I was bucking tradition, but I knew I was right.

This particular Kielian snake was sound asleep. I turned to Lillium. "Did it ever strike you that perhaps Kielian snakes could be more than just a surface to eat from or honers in the honing pit, Lillium?"

"Just call me Lil, please." She blinked prettily and I felt a little riffle in my gizzard.

---

17 Nest-maid snakes had the capacity to extend their bodies and serve as tables when there was the space. In family hollows, which were small, they were rarely used in this way. But in institutional settings, the practice was often implemented as it was a very efficient way of dining.

"What would you propose, old fellow?" said Cadet Skellig. "Want them to be flight instructors?"

Lil churred softly, then spoke. "Well, they don't have wings, but their heads are very strong. They did hollow out our barracks, after all."

"No brains, my dear!" Skellig laughed. "No brains at all!"

"Shush!" Lil said. "She can hear you."

Skellig brushed her off. "She's sound asleep. You can't wake her up!" He took a talon and dragged it across the snake's scales.

"Don't do that!" Lil nearly spat.

"Don't fret. She didn't budge. These old gals have tough hides," Skellig said.

"It's disrespectful," I said rather sharply.

"Sorry, old fellow, but I don't think respect is the point."

I was aghast at this remark. Suddenly, I didn't like Cadet Skellig calling me "old fellow" anymore. How could such a good-natured owl suddenly seem so . . . so ill-natured, so cynical?

"It's exactly the point," I countered. "We should respect Kielian snakes. The snakes could do a lot more than we ask them to."

"Oh, dear," Skellig said, suddenly contrite. "Look, I'm sorry, really. I had a bad experience as an owlet with a Kielian snake."

"You did?" Thora said. She was sitting at the tail end of the snake and had been silent until this point.

"Yes, it was really awful, quite horrendous. She stabbed me with her fangs."

"Great Glaux!" Lil said.

"Indeed. Here's the wound." Skellig lifted his starboard wing, and just where it joined the upper part of his body, there was a bare patch with a ragged scar. "It's healed now. But it was touch-and-go for a while. She was a mad old thing, but still." He paused. "It was stupid of me to bring my personal experience to the table." He stroked the nest-maid rather gently with his wing tip. She slept on.

CHAPTER 15

What Thora Saw

I have to admit that I found Skellig's apology, well — touching, for lack of a better word. And sincere. Apparently, Thora was not so quick to forgive. She returned to the barracks after our twixt-time repast, troubled not just so much by Skellig's harsh words, but by the wound beneath his starboard wing. It was not a wound made by snake fangs. Of this, she told me later, she was certain. The puckered skin bore all the marks of a siege blade, one of the most difficult of all blades to forge. Where would a young owl like Skellig have encountered such a blade? He was a cadet. He had seen no action.

When Cadet Skellig snuck out in late morning to the grog trees, Thora decided to follow him. She would be discreet and lag a good way behind him. There were some puffy clouds overhead that would provide camouflage for her if necessary. She knew Skellig was not a particularly skillful flier, so she had no fear of keeping up with him. But Thora blinked, because as soon as Skellig was out of the barracks, he went into a beautiful, steep banking turn and headed for the isolated cliffs at the far end of Dark Fowl, a place known for its tumultuous winds. He laid on the speed, negotiating the turbulence with a grace she had never seen before from him.

Thora began to feel a kind of blackening dread in her gizzard. Cumulus clouds were building up just south of the point, and she decided to bury herself in them and listen. Skellig's flying was still not as silent as most, perhaps because of his wound, so she could track him fairly easily. Soon, she picked up another sound, quite distinct. From the whisper of the wind passing over its plummels,[20] she could tell there was a Pygmy Owl in the cloud bank as well. She heard a faint churr when the two of them met up, and then the Pygmy turned and flew straight out to sea. Cadet Skellig curved around on a flight path, Thora guessed, toward the grog tree favored by Orf. Listening carefully, Thora could tell that there was something different in Cadet Skellig's flight. He was flying heavier. Was he carrying a weapon? But no. It didn't sound that heavy. A botkin of some sort? Thora tipped her head and contracted her facial disc to home in on the sound.

From the way the wind whistled against it, Thora could tell the object Skellig was carrying was not made from metal. It seemed instead to be made from something soft and slightly

---

20 Small owls such as Pygmy, Elf, and Northern Saw-whets, unlike the majority of owls, lack fringe feathers, or what we call plummels, to quiet their flight. They are inherently noisy fliers.

furry. Moleskins were often used by field medics for transporting powders and unguents for wounds. It must be a moleskin. But if Cadet Skellig needed medicine for his wound, which looked well healed, why wouldn't he just go to the Academy infirmary?

All this was becoming more and more mysterious, and Thora was determined to find out what was happening. It was still quite early. Owls tended to rest up a bit before hitting the grog trees, and Orf in particular had quite a bit of work to do to dampen his forge at the end of the night. He was meticulous about his tools, and he always started a load of cold coals braising in the moss-lined ice cubbies before he left.

Thora hid herself in the snow-laden boughs of a bushy spruce tree and watched Skellig landing in the grog tree a short distance away. As she suspected, the grog tree wasn't open for business yet. Tin cups hung on the pegs unattended. Each smith had their own cup with their mark inscribed on it. Thora watched carefully as Skellig approached the branch with the cups, but couldn't see what he was doing. Something didn't feel right to her, not at all.

The grog keeper finally appeared.

"Well, ain't you the early bird, Cadet!"

"I like to be here when the troops arrive," Skellig said. "I learn more from them than I do in any class."

"Probably right. Now what'll it be, bingle or bangle?"[21]

"Oh, bangle. Like to be able to think straight, you know."

"Got a lot to think about, eh?"

Skellig suddenly looked a bit nervous, as if he had said too much. "Not really. But I like to be alert for the stories."

"Here you go." The grog keeper set out a cup of bangle juice.

By this time, a few more owls had shown up. There were two smiths from down island and then three battle-weary Burrowing Owls back from the front, one with a patch over his eye.

"A double-strength bingle shot will help you with that," the keeper said, nodding at the owl with the eye patch.

Two enormous Eagle Owls arrived and perched a bit away from the others. Skellig looked around as if expecting someone, but seemed to assiduously avoid the gaze of the Eagle Owls.

"Hail, Orf," the keeper hooted, and a hooray went up in the tree.

"Here at last!" said a Barn Owl, though one might not have guessed his species, for his white, heart-shaped face was so streaked with soot it looked nearly black.

---

[21] Bangle juice is unfermented bingle juice, thus without any alcohol. Grog keepers are notoriously lax about serving alcoholic beverages to cadets.

"I was wrestling with cold fire and cold coals. Takes a while but it's the season, as you know," Orf offered.

"You braising already?" the Barn owl asked.

"Ayuh, the best time is when the weather starts to change. The dampness locks in the chill." He sighed and leaned forward on his perch toward the keep. "Gimme a bingle with a touch of bangle, Jobee. Need to start off with a bit of the soft stuff."

"Coming right up, sir."

Thora couldn't take her eyes off Orf. She worshipped the smith. In her mind, he was more than a blacksmith, more than a weapons monger. He was an artist. Everything he did seemed artistic to Thora — the way he wielded his hammer, the way he held his tongs. Even the way he sipped his juice was special, interesting.

It wasn't long before the grog tree was crowded. A gadfeather arrived and began to sing a bawdy song:

> Me and my mate
> We got a date
> At the old grog tree tonight.
> She used to drink bangle
> But I got her to bingle,
> And you know what happened then!
> For I drank the bingle

And now I ain't single,
So let's drink and drink again.
I got my cup hanging in the old grog tree,
She's got her cup right beside me.
We'll bingle the bangle
And jangle the jingle,
Then I'll fly into the night
With my heart's delight.
And come the morn
Back to the tree again,
Where our cups await
And we've got a date.
We'll start all over again.

The songs got bawdier with "Tickle Me Tail Feathers." Then romantic — "Got a Lot of Love in This Old Gizzard." Then the owls sang a rousing fight song:

Hail, hail, warriors valiant,
We'll conquer them yet.
With our banners flying,
We'll pursue them to their deaths!
For we are warriors of Kiel.
We don't give in,
We don't give up.

We fight to the end
And never bend.
Now let's raise a cup!

Thora saw Orf lift a talon to his brow as if he were tired or perhaps suffering from a headache. She was downwind of the tree slightly and tipped her head so she could better pick up what he was saying to the keeper.

"Feeling poorly, Orf?" the keeper asked.

"A bit of a headache. Often happens this time a year when I'm braising the cold coals. The fumes, you know. Think I'll be toddling off."

It looked more like toddling to Thora than actual flying. Orf flew only a short distance before settling down and trying to get lift again. Thora noticed that he was heading in the opposite direction of his forge, as if he was completely disoriented. She was about to fly out from her spot in the boughs of the fir tree to see if he needed help, when she saw that the two Eagle Owls had flipped their heads around and were following Orf's progress. There was a lot of boisterous singing and tumult in the tree by this time, and no one noticed the Eagle Owls leave with Skellig.

Thora felt dread building in her gizzard. She knew that Orf was in danger but the two immense Eagle Owls were not birds to trifle with. They were at least twice her size and three times her wingspan. *The perfect wingspan for . . . Oh, great Glaux!* It suddenly dawned on her. They were planning a transport vacuum![22]

Two more Eagle Owls materialized out of a heavily boughed fir tree just like the one she had been hiding in. Should she scream? Sound an alarm? The owls in the grog tree were too far into the bingle juice to do anything. Should she go back and fetch the others, Lyze, Moss? It was too far and in the opposite direction. Orf would be gone by then.

Thora made a quick decision — she would have to track the Eagle Owls. When she knew where they had taken Orf, she could report back and get help. She was sure they would not kill Orf; his knowledge was too valuable. His cold coals and the ice weapons were superior to anything existing in the Northern Kingdoms. Those weapons alone were responsible for more deaths on the battlefield than any others. Of course the Ice Talons League wanted Orf! They would force him to make his cold weapons and the hot ones as well — the fizblisters, the flails, the ice daggers.

Then it struck Thora. All the times she went to observe Orf working at his forge, who was always there? Cadet Skellig! And this wasn't the first time she had seen Skellig at a grog tree

---

22 A transport vacuum is a method for transporting wounded owls or prisoners in flight. It is a windless chamber formed by four owls arranged in a diamond configuration. The transport vacuum was invented in the Northern Kingdoms and called a kronkenbot. It would not be used extensively in the Southern Kingdoms until the wars with the Pure Ones.

favored by Orf. She had assumed that Skellig was interested in smithing, just like herself. But she remembered Skellig questioning Orf carefully about when the season for the cold coals would start. Now she knew it was because Skellig wanted to know when to nab him. Skellig must have put a potion in Orf's cup. That accounted for Orf's staggering flight from the grog tree. It was no headache from braising cold coals. They had drugged him!

The weather had turned dirty. Clouds rolled in from the north, and the day darkened. There was a mixture of snow, sleet, and hail — perfect weather for making cold coals. The dense cloud cover provided good camouflage for Thora, but she began to worry. She could clearly hear the Eagle Owls talking, but the sound of Orf's breathing, his heart, and the gurgles of his gizzard were growing dimmer and dimmer. Had they given him too much of the drug? Was Orf dying?

CHAPTER 16

A Strategy Is Planned

"What? What are you saying?" I asked Thora as she shook me awake.

Moss heard her and began to rouse himself.

"It's high noon, for Glaux's sake! What are you doing up at this hour! Have you been drinking the bingle or something?"

"No! No! Come out of the barracks. I have to tell you something — privately!"

Grumbling, Moss and I followed Thora outside. "What is it?" Moss said grouchily. This was one owl who did not like to be wakened.

"Orf — they've owl-knapped him," she said quietly. Our beaks dropped open.

There was dead silence.

"We've got to tell someone," I said. "We better alert the regimental commander."

"No!" Thora said sharply.

"Why not?" Moss asked.

"There were three other owls, Eagle Owls like the ones who took him, circling around the Academy headquarters and the parliament hollow — well-camouflaged, since the weather stinks." She tipped her head up at the dark thunderheads hammering across the sky. Hag clouds, we called them. Lightning forked from them like the gnarled talons of a hagsfiend. Seagulls clattered into the sky, seeking refuge from the tumultuous sea.

"They know," Thora continued with her head tipped toward the sky. "The owls know that when it's discovered that Orf is missing, an all-out search will be launched. A squadron." Thora looked at me. "Those Eagle Owls over the parliament will report it immediately."

"A squadron isn't right for this. It's too unwieldly," I said. In my short time at the Academy, I had learned a thing or two. The one thing that the Academy lacked — indeed, the whole Kielian League lacked — were units with what I thought of as extreme maneuverability. We were fighting an old war, a century-long war, with old tactics. We needed new strategies and we needed them fast — like now! If just a few of us went, we could slip in unnoticed, as a squadron never could.

Thora nodded at us. "Then let's claw up."

"Lil — we need her," I said. "There is nobody better with a hot lance than Lil."

They knew I was right. Lil had become a fantastic lancer.

It was as if Lil was out to prove to Lud-Dud that she was no missy when it came to fighting. She had exhibited such skills that she had won the coveted retractable hot lance in the full-shine games that were held when the moon was at its brightest.

"She'll bring Miss Hot Point!" Moss exclaimed. They had all been shocked when Lil had given her hot lance this odd nickname. Lil had a wicked sense of humor, and it was her way of getting back at Lud-Dud and showing him just what a Miss Cadet could do with the right weapon in her talons.

The owls who had nabbed Orf had taken him to Elsemere Island, an exceedingly clever move because it was the home of the Glauxian Sisters, a nonviolent meditative order that had taken vows of silence. The one exception to their rule of silence was in treating the sick or wounded. Then they could speak. They were renowned for their skills in the healing arts. The sisters were so peaceful that they didn't hunt. They existed on little more than kelp and any creatures caught in the seaweed. Snails and bivalves such as clams or oysters were fine for them, for they had no blood.

Thora said the Eagle Owls and Skellig had taken Orf to the cliffs on the opposite side of the island from where the sisters lived, about as far from their retreat as possible. And even if the sisters had known that the Ice Talon operatives had nabbed the greatest blacksmith in the Northern Kingdoms, what would they have been able to say? The sisters didn't believe in war or weapons. They had stayed neutral throughout the hundred-year history of this war and welcomed all owls to their infirmary for treatment, no matter what side they were on.

Our fear was that Elsemere Island was an interim stop for the treacherous owls. They would undoubtedly move on, skirting the northernmost coast of the Southern Kingdoms, and then head straight for the heart of Ice Talons League territory.

As we approached the island, Lil turned to me. Her eyes glowed such a bright gold in the full sun of the day that I felt a shiver pass through my gizzard. Was this love? I couldn't think of such things now.

"You realize what's at stake here?" Lil began. "If we fail, we'll all be de-commed and thrown out of the Academy, but more important, the war will be over. The Ice Talons League will win. They're already stronger than we are, and with Orf they'll have all the best weapons, too."

I knew this, and I had but one thought: *We cannot fail!*

CHAPTER 17

The Deadly Sisters

As we approached the northeast side of the island, we spotted a few of the sisters below us skimming the kelp beds in a small inlet. Others were combing the beach. They wore snoods on the backs of their heads and, falling to their shoulders, a kind of ornamental net woven from the lacy seaweed native to the island. Across their faces, they draped veils of the same seaweed, but with large eye-openings so they could see.

"I don't know how they fly with that stuff hanging all over them," Lil said.

"They probably wonder how we fly with battle claws," Moss replied.

"Look!" Lil said, flipping her head up. "There's an honest-to-Glaux smee hole above the cliffs where they have Orf!"

I felt a sudden tingle in my gizzard. "If that's the case, silence!"

I gave the wing waggle signal. Although we hadn't quite mastered the code, I did my best to explain a strategy with it.

We would soar on the updrafts of the steam vents directly over the cave and listen in on the Ice Talon operatives. Steam, like water and air, transmits sound beautifully. Despite my far-from-perfect signaling, the other three owls immediately grasped what I was saying. So we swooped into the smee hole and soon could pick up the voices of the duplicitous owls of the Ice Talons League.

Skellig's voice gave us a shock. He sounded older, more mature, and spoke with a clipped assurance. The Great Horned was no cadet, but a seasoned commander. Great Glaux, my gizzard swelled with loathing for him.

"I think he's coming around," Skellig said. "I put just enough powder in his cup to get him here. Maybe we can get something out of him."

Orf didn't sound like himself, either. He was decidedly groggy but alive — his heart was definitely beating. I could see the relief in everyone's eyes. Still, Skellig's words made my gizzard flinch — *We can get something out of him.* He must mean the formula for cold coals. And if they got it out of him, would they kill him? We had thought they were going to capture Orf and bring him to their armory to begin forging. But it sounded as if they only wanted the formula.

But what assurance did they have that Orf would give them the real formula? Had Skellig learned enough in his observations to be able to discern the real one from a fake?

"We'll get him to that abandoned forge on the far side of Stormfast," one of the Eagle Owls said.

At this, I thought Thora was going to go kerplonken. Her forge, her secret forge! Once there, they would test the formula, and if it worked, they would kill Orf. If it didn't, they would torture him until he gave them the right formula.

We had to get out of the smee-hole draft. We had to talk and not be heard. I gave a slight wing tap to Moss, who was flying next to me, and made a quick exit. The others followed. We roosted up on the west side of Elsemere, downwind of the cave. They couldn't hear us.

"We have to act fast," Thora said. "I'll bet you anything they pilfered cold coals from someone, if not Orf then another smith of Dark Fowl. Skellig himself probably did it."

I thought of that moleskin pouch that Thora had told us about in which Skellig had carried the powders to drug Orf. He could have used one just like it to carry cold coals. They might have withered a bit but they could be revived if someone knew what they were doing. "Once Orf has been forced to show them how to forge a weapon with cold coals, they'll kill him on the spot. We have to think of something," I said. Everyone was listening to me except for Lil, who was looking off toward the beach below where we were perched. She had begun to peel off her battle claws.

"What are you doing?" Thora asked.

"I have an idea. You and me, Thora, we have to get down to that beach and get some seaweed."

"Whatever for?"

"We're sisters."

"Huh?" Thora said. Moss and I blinked.

"Glauxian Sisters! We're going to make ourselves some snoods and veils and take vows of silence, except to give succor to the wounded. And there's one other rule here — nonviolence. But not us! We're going to be deadly — the deadliest sisters on this island."

"Hellooooo!" Lil trilled in the sweet tones of a very elderly owl. "Sister Alymisia here."

"And Sister Pollifer!" Thora added. "We believe you have a wounded soldier with you?"

"Everything's fine," one of the Eagle Owls replied.

"Oh! We thought we saw a vacuum transport?"

"It's nothing to worry about," Skellig said.

"No, we're doing quite fine in here," said another of the Eagle Owls, poking his head out of the cave. He was unclawed and his bare talons showed.

An agonizing cry of pain punctured the air.

"Oh, dear!" Lil exclaimed in a hoarse voice. "That doesn't sound fine to me. Does it, Sister Pollifer?"

She gave a slight nod, and the two owls charged into the cave. Before the Skellig and the Eagle Owls knew what had happened, Lil had drawn out Miss Hot Point, her hot lance, and hurled it. The lance pierced Skellig's starboard wing.

"Let me finish the damage done by the nest-maid snake! Or was it a siege blade?" Lil screeched. The pile of feathers that was Orf sprang to life. He seized a pair of battle claws that lay discarded and lashed out at an Eagle Owl, raking its eyes from its face. Thora jousted with a half scimitar of her own design.

Moss and I flew into the cave, both of us armed with ice. The one Eagle Owl, now blinded, was no longer in contention, but there were still three more Eagle Owls. One fully clawed, one half clawed, and one bare taloned. We needed to get them into the air where we could fight better and where we would have the advantage because they didn't have any weapons. Or so we thought, until the half-clawed eagle produced a flail and began whirling it overhead. He was aiming at Lil, who was trying to retrieve Miss Hot Point from Skellig's shattered and bloody wing.

"Lil, leave it!" I shouted. She ducked just in time. The flail swung by her and hit a target all right — Skellig! It split his skull neatly in half. Orf stepped up and extricated the flail from the bloody pulp of what had been Skellig's head.

"All right, you contemptible old grotter, you!" Orf swung the flail with an ease and grace unlike anything I had ever seen. He was vastly superior to any of our instructors. Of course, Orf had designed the weapon and knew it like no other owl. The Eagle Owls beat a hasty retreat, streaking out of the cave. And that was where the real surprise happened.

In the vanishing light of the day, as the sky became tinged with what owls call First Lavender, two owls emerged out of the clouds — one huge and the other tiny. It was Loki and Blix, the Great Gray and the Northern Saw-whet. I saw something slice through the air like the tail of an infinitesimally small comet. There was a spurt of very red blood, heart's blood, and one of the Eagle Owls plummeted. What aim! Another comet flew by, thrown by Blix almost immediately after the first.

Great Glaux! I thought. Loki and Blix were doing exactly what I had imagined. A midair reload! Loki was carrying a quiver of ice splinters, and Blix launched them one after another. We began to fight with renewed vigor. This was not a squadron, not a platoon, nor even a brigade, but exactly what I dreamed of — a hyper-maneuverable unit of owls of mixed sizes who were all fighting at the knife edge of our skills. The battle was over as fast as it had begun.

"Fetch up! Fetch up!" Orf shouted, and we flew to the roosting place where we had originally planned out the assault.

I was breathless not just from the combat, but from the overwhelming surprise of Loki and Blix's arrival.

"Where — where did you come from?" I stammered. We were all shocked.

Loki explained. "Orf was discovered missing just after midday. Then you four and Skellig . . ."

"By the way, where is Skellig?" Blix asked.

"Dead."

"Oh, dear!" Blix gasped.

"Don't waste your tears," Lil said.

Blix grimaced. "It looked like he might have been in on this. Someone said they saw him snitch cold coals. But when you four turned up missing, too — they were ready to blame you as well."

"Us!" Thora said indignantly.

"Especially you, Thora. They said you were always hanging around Orf's forge," Loki added.

"Well, she was!" Orf explained. "Don't blame Thora. If it hadn't been for Thora . . ." Orf's voice dwindled as if he couldn't contemplate the fate he had escaped.

"If it hadn't been for Thora, none of us would be here," I cut in. "But how did you and Loki ever find us?"

"One of the gadfeathers — I don't think those owls ever sleep — she said she thought she saw the four of you fly off. Loki and I were so upset. They're going to de-comm you from the Academy!"

CHAPTER 18

An Odd Welcome

Did we return to glory? Not precisely, for even though we had rescued Orf, our methods were looked upon as dubious. The air was thick with the suspicions of the old-timers like Lud-Dud and his friends. An Elf Owl, Colonel Stellan Micrathene Whitneyi, the instructor of the B unit of the Frost Beaks, was outraged that Blix took not one, but: "Five! Count them, Blix, five ice splinters!"

"But I only used three, Colonel Stellan Micrathene Whitneyi. And those hit their mark. One even got heart's blood."

"I don't give a bloody racdrop about heart's blood," she ranted. "You took ice splinters from the armory without using the proper sign-out procedure. And I'm not even sure how you carried them all."

"Oh! Colonel, I can explain that," I offered.

"Shut up, Cadet Lyze Megascops!" Lud-Dud thundered.

If Orf had been there, he would have jumped to our defense. But he had been hustled off to high command for a debriefing.

So we were subjected to a scorching reprimand. Our rescue of Orf took a back wing to the innumerable rules we had violated, which our superiors were only too willing to trot out one by one, ad yarpium.

"Number one," Optimus Strix Varia, the regimental commander, began, "you were all absent without leave. AWOL!" he roared. "Number two, you initiated a combat mission without consulting your commanding officer. Number three . . ."

On and on he went. I was dying to interrupt and say, "Number four, we got Orf back, you idiotic old fogies!" I wanted to explain how brilliant Blix and Loki had been. I wanted to describe the midair reload. I wanted to tell them Thora's idea for a new kind of quiver to make reloading even easier.

Orf returned from his debriefing and listened carefully and with obvious surprise to the sharp criticism we were taking. By this time, the regimental commander had almost exhausted his venomous lecture and was becoming slightly more conciliatory. "Well, Cadets, I hope you have learned your lesson," Optimus Strix Varia sighed wearily.

"Lesson! What lesson?" Orf growled. "We are the ones who need to learn some lessons here. What these young'uns did out there was nothing short of brilliant. I've just cleared it with the speaker of the parliament, General Andricus Tyto Alba. Cadet Thora is no longer to be in training as a combat cadet."

"I told you so," snickered Colonel Stellan Micrathene Whitneyi. "They're de-comming her."

"I heard that, Colonel," Orf roared. "Nothing of the sort! Thora is to serve as a cadet apprentice to me."

"A female blacksmith?" A murmur rose among the commanding officers.

"Insane," someone whispered.

"Strains credulity," Lud-Dud hissed.

"Don't strain that wee brain of yours too hard, Captain Ludvigsen Asio Flammeus. We wouldn't want a cranial rupture," Orf muttered. Flapping his wings noisily, he turned to Thora and said, "Follow me, Cadet Apprentice Thora Nyctea Scandiaca." This was somewhat extraordinary. Orf had just addressed Thora by her full species name, a sign of the highest respect. A silence fell in the hollow. Colonel Stellan and the others seemed to wilf and meekly parted way as the blacksmith marched through the crowd. Thora herself seemed stunned.

Orf glared at Lud-Dud and Stellan and the others as he passed, but he smiled when he stopped in front of me. "Lyze." He nodded, turning to Lil, Blix, and Loki as well. "General Andricus wishes to meet with you. Thora, you too. All five of you follow me."

I thought I heard a snicker from Lud-Dud, as if to hint that finally we were to get our comeuppance. I have to admit I thought the same, and as we entered the general's hollow, my gizzard was aquiver.

General Andricus Tyto Alba was a strikingly handsome owl except for a scar that ran down his breast. It was said an ice splinter had come within inches of his heart in a battle in the high H'rath, years before. He had fought on fiercely, though blood had poured from his chest. The general was quite large for a Barn Owl and some said had the strength of an Eagle Owl, the largest of all owls. Stern, uncompromising, he was not one to suffer fools or cowards.

His back was toward us as we entered, but he wheeled about. The scar blazed across his chest in a diagonal slash. It was shocking to look at, and I couldn't help but wonder how the attack had missed his heart. How he could have survived such a wound?

"And what do you cadets plan to do for your summer holidays?" the general asked. "You certainly deserve a holiday!" I could feel everyone's relief. We were not going to be punished.

"Thora and I hope to go to the Shagdah Snurl with Blix and Loki, sir," I replied.

"I'm not sure what I plan to do," Moss answered.

"Oh, great Glaux, I nearly forgot!" The general swiveled his head toward me. "Cadet Lyze Megascops, a message for you was delivered by your aunt Hanja. She says that you are expected home. A new home, as I understand your family hollow was destroyed. Let's see . . . Sergeant Alion Tyto Castanops?" he called out. The general's secretary, a Masked Owl, came forward.

"Yes, sir." The sergeant saluted crisply.

"Do you have the note left by his aunt?"

"Right here, sir."

"Let me see it."

The general took out a pair of issen blauen spectacles. Thinner than the combat goggles, they magnified his eyes enormously as he began to read the piece of birch bark. "Says here that your family has relocated to a hollow on the northern side of Stormfast — up an inlet in a grove of spruce trees. They expect you home for . . . oh, my goodness! A blessed event — your mum seems to have laid an egg, and they will be in residence most of the summer."

"Oh," I said quietly.

"What marvelous news!" the general boomed.

"Yes," I replied in a subdued voice. But in truth I was rather disappointed. I hadn't really finished grieving for Lysa. How could Lysa be replaced so easily? I supposed that's how it was in the owl world, especially when we had been at war for a century. We were always told we must forge on. If a parent died, the remaining mate usually found a new partner quickly. It was simply our way. We had to move forward.

But I was not quite ready to forge on. And I really wanted to go to the Shagdah Snurl with Blix, Loki, and Thora. I wanted to see how the winds hatched. I wanted to feel their furl as they were birthed out in the coldest place on Earth by the hot tentacles that snaked out from the volcano and its lava lake in the mysterious Nacht Sted. I wanted to see that lake where rock melted. It was a place of legend, but I knew legends were born from unrevealed truths. Legends tell stories about forces we sometimes cannot understand but are part of the fabric of our lives. I so wanted to go, but it was not to be.

As I was leaving, the general stopped me. "Wait a minute, lad. I have a question for you."

"Yes, sir?"

"Orf told me that you have some notions, some ideas about . . . well . . . how should I put it? Newfangled ways of fighting. You did pretty well out there at Elsemere. Apparently, this midair reload was something to behold."

"I had mentioned the idea to Blix and Loki, sir, but they really figured it out. They should get the credit."

"When you return, I'd be most pleased if you would come visit me again and share any other ideas you might have."

"Really, sir?" I squeaked.

"Yes, really." He opened his eyes wide and blinked behind the issen blauen spectacles. "Want to give me a hint as to one or two of those ideas now?"

My heart raced, my gizzard quickened. This was a rare opportunity. The instructors at the Academy never listened to cadets. How could I forget Captain Lud-Dud's accusations that I was being too fanciful? And now that was just what the general was asking me to be. Within the space of a minute, my existence, my life, took on new meaning.

"Sir, have you ever thought of including Kielian snakes in a combat unit?"

"Kielian snakes?" He shoved his head forward and removed his spectacles. "Great Glaux, no! It rather boggles the mind."

"Not mine," I replied. "I think they're underutilized."

The general considered. "Come up with a plan and I'll hear you out."

"Absolutely, sir."

I have to admit that my spirits were lifted considerably. The prospect of going home and not to the Shagdah Snurl was less grim. Now my main concern was how much I would miss Lil. I already had an ache in my heart and a soreness in my gizzard. My first season at the Kielian Military Academy had drawn to a close. I would return when the first snows of liffen schmoo began to fall and, by the following spring, I would be a commissioned officer in the Allied Forces of the Kielian League.

CHAPTER 19

A New Hollow and a New Owlet

Our new hollow was in a stand of stout blue spruce. I could imagine that in the winter when the snow stayed fast on the ground, it would be lovely. This type of spruce, as its name indicates, has a bluish tinge, and the shadow it casts would fall like a blue filigree net on the white snow. By the time I arrived, my new brother, Ifghar, had hatched. Like many owlets that hatch at this time of year, he was advanced. Summer chicks tend to be that way. The hunting is good, so they grow faster. He was fledging out nicely, but all right, I'll admit it right here: He did not capture my heart the way Lysa had. But he was a good little fellow and he worshipped me.

Mum and Da seemed fine. One morning toward twixt time, I remembered something very clever and funny that Lysa had said about the sun just as it was rising.

"Mum, Da," I said. "Once at twixt time, Lysa peeked out the hollow and said that the sun reminded her of a —" But the words died on my beak because both my parents swiveled their heads toward me and glared.

"Never mind," I whispered. It was clear that I was not ever to mention Lysa, the old hollow, or even Gundesfyrr again. Lingering emotions were considered a sign of weakness among seasoned soldiers of the Kielian League. There had been a period of mourning, and they believed that prolonging it served no purpose. It was as if that part of our lives had been sealed off forever.

Oddly enough, it wasn't until I had been there for nearly an entire day and night that I thought of Gilda. I was shocked that I had not noticed her absence. Perhaps I, too, had begun to seal off those memories. Before I could stop myself, a question slid out.

"Mum, what happened to Gilda?"

"Oh, I let her go."

"Let her go! How could you? She saved my life."

"Well, she wasn't a very good housekeeper. I felt I could do it better. She was very distractible. I think nest-maiding wasn't really in her . . . how should I put it . . . her skill set?"

I nearly exploded. I wanted to say, *You're darned right, it wasn't.* Gilda was a fighter, a warrior if I ever saw one.

My mum continued, "I felt I could take care of this new hollow as well as any nest-maid snake."

My mother was betraying a sudden streak of domesticity that was completely unlike her. The first thing she had announced upon my arrival was that she'd had no broody for

Ifghar. She seemed enormously proud of having brooded him herself. I dared not ask if she was contemplating retirement.

My father was not considering any such thing. Indeed, he was called back to the front on the eve of Ifghar's First-Meat-on-Bones ceremony. At dawn before he left, Da and I went out to hunt for rockmunks, which were at their tenderest this time of year and perfect for Ifghar. Their flesh has an almost creamy consistency.

Mum had a funny light in her eye as she greeted us on the branch outside when we returned. A familiar trill issued forth from deep in the hollow.

"But look who's here!" My gizzard locked. It was Tantya Hanja. "I'm just in time," she said, waddling forth. No wonder my mum had that odd look in her eye. "One family member has to leave, but another arrives. Nothing like having family about when it comes to these ceremonies!" Tantya Hanja cackled.

"But I want my da," whined Ifghar.

"He'll be here for the ceremony, dear," my mother said.

"But then he'll have to leave right after," Ifghar complained.

"I am here, darling lad," Tantya Hanja said. "I know all the songs."

"I don't like the way you sing. It hurts my ear slits."

"Ifghar! Shame on you," Mum scolded. But I nearly laughed out loud.

It was not the jolliest of ceremonies, although we all did our best. I kept thinking about Gilda and wishing she had been there. She always told such good stories. Who cared about her skills as a nest-maid?

A very nice Barred Owl family and another family of Barn Owls stopped in. Moss, bless his soul, showed up at the last minute with his three sisters, who had grown into lovely lasses and would be returning to the Academy with us come autumn.

I noticed that everyone perched as far away as possible from Tantya Hanja. I found myself actually feeling sorry for her. Once upon a time she'd had a mate, but he died rather young. She led a very lonely life. Some say that she had attempted to be a gadfeather, but her voice was such that she never had a real following. The one time she had attended the yearly spring equinox gathering of gadfeathers, she performed to an audience of one, an elderly Whiskered Screech who had seemed quite besotted by her but had dropped dead within hours of hearing her sing. That fixed her reputation not simply as a terrible singer, but as an ill-omened owl.

Thinking about all this depressed me greatly, especially as I hadn't received any messages from Lil since I had returned home. Every day I looked for a Great Horned Owl messenger. Great Horneds were most often messenger owls, for they flew the fastest of all of us. I also looked for a falcon, just in case. Falcons can fly twice as fast as any owl,[23] but were generally reserved for military messaging.

I had written to Lil once but hadn't received any reply and was uncertain if I should write to her again. I didn't want to seem too eager, but I *was* eager, darn it! Four days after Ifghar's Meat-on-Bones ceremony, I couldn't help myself and took a charred twig to begin to scratch something out on a piece of birch bark.

"What'cha doing?" Ifghar asked, trying to perch beside me.

"What does it look like I'm doing?"

"Writing a letter."

"That's right."

"Who to?" Ifghar could be a little annoying at times. And once he started asking questions, they multiplied endlessly.

"A friend."

"What kind of friend?"

"Just somebody I met at the Academy!"

"What kind of somebody?"

"Really, Ifghar! How can I write if you keep interrupting me?"

"Quit pestering Lyze, Ifghar. Come help me tuck in this rabbit's ear moss."

---

23 Great Horned Owls can attain speeds of up to forty leagues an hour. But Peregrine Falcons can fly twice that speed.

"I bet it's a girlfriend!" Ifghar hooted. "Ha-ha-ha! Lyze has a girlfriend! Lyze has a girlfriend!" He began to dance around the hollow chanting this annoying refrain.

"Why don't you just go outside and announce it to the whole world!" I exploded.

"I think I will."

He had just started branching and was quite full of himself. He had taken right to it. I could hear him outside hopping about. Then suddenly, he gasped. "Mum, a messenger's coming!"

I was out of the hollow in no time and flew up to where Ifghar had perched. My gizzard was thumping. It was a Great Horned with a scroll in his talons.

"I would have been here sooner, but this was passed on to me. The falcon was . . . er, intercepted." I felt a twinge of anguish.

"Is — is it for me?"

The Great Horned looked at me narrowly. "Not unless you're Major Ulfa Megascops Trichopsis."

Oh, great Glaux, I thought, trying to still my gizzard. "No, I'm not," I said softly. "I'll get her."

My mum took the scroll with trembling talons. I didn't need to hear the news — we both knew what a scroll like this meant.

Her beak quivered as she read the words: " 'Dear Major Ulfa Megascops Trichopsis, it saddens me to inform you that your mate, General Raskin Megascops Trichopsis, supreme commander of the Kielian League, fell in battle in the H'rath Range two nights ago. General Rask died serving his league valiantly. He took an ice sword straight to the gizzard.'"

Death had touched us again. First Edvard, then Lysa, and now my da. Death bears with it a stain that seeps into the hollow and fills the mind. Those first days when dawn came and I tried to sleep while hearing the soft mewling of my mother, my thoughts were streaked with memories of Da and me together and our wonderful flight to the Hock. It was all I could think about. In my dreams, it was my father who flew into the sea smoke and seemed to dissolve before my eyes as the smoke thickened. The dreamscape merged with the suffocating smoke of the fiery pine from the night when Lysa died. The haunting scent of the sweet, boiling sap suffused my dreams, almost like the scroom of the tree.

That smell had clung to my feathers for days after Lysa's death. I remember being so glad when I molted that season, for at last the cloying odor was gone. But now it came back again to haunt my dreams — my dreams of death.

My mother became deeply morose and, as the nights passed, only seemed to be getting worse. Until this point, my experience with grief had been limited to Lysa's death. I had known Lysa for just a few scant moons, and I couldn't imagine how difficult it must be to lose a mate you had known for countless moons, for years. Mum became so quiet and so unresponsive to Ifghar, who was a demanding little owlet, that I asked her if it might not be a good idea to get a new nest-maid snake. Mum seemed obsessed with trailing around the nest and cleaning up vermin.

"No!" she said. "I need something to keep me busy."

"Don't I keep you busy?" Ifghar asked plaintively.

"Oh, Ifghar, you have Lyze," she said, trying to sound cheerful. "He's teaching you wonderful things. How's your flying coming along?"

"He says I'll soon be ready to fly to the Hock."

I couldn't wait until he was ready, for I really wanted to try to find Hoke. I had not stopped thinking about my ideas, or how General Andricus Tyto Alba had encouraged me to think about what he called the "newfangled ways of fighting." One evening, when my mother's silence lay as thick as brikta schnee in the middle of winter and I felt I couldn't stand it one more minute, I turned to her.

"Mum," I said, flipping my head around to where she was distractedly petting some of Ifghar's new feathers. "When I was at the Academy, I had . . . had —" I wasn't sure how to begin.

"Had what?" Ifghar said. "A girlfriend?" he said, smirking. I remember wondering how a little owlet knew how to smirk. It felt unseemly in one so young.

"No, Ifghar," I snapped. "I had some ideas about warfare."

My mum blinked. "Really, dear?" It was the first time since the news of Da's death that I had seen a genuine sparkle in her eye. It illuminated our hollow like a blast of sunlight.

"Yes, Mum, and General Andricus Tyto Alba encouraged me to come up with more over the break."

"Andricus himself! Well, tell me about it." She turned to my brother. "Don't interrupt as you often do. Try to listen, Ifghar."

I took a deep breath. "Mum, how big is your commando unit, the Ice Daggers?"

"Twenty owls."

"All Whiskered Screeches?"

"No, a couple of Barn Owls."

"But generally, what you would call midsized owls."

"Yes, definitely. Midsized owls are best with Ice Daggers. That's what a commando unit is, after all: a specialized unit composed of owls who are skillful with certain weapons." She paused and looked at me. "Why all these questions?"

"What if we redefine specialized to still mean focused, but include a mixture of owls of different sizes that excel with more than just one weapon?"

"You're losing me here."

I had blessedly lost Ifghar, too, for he had fallen sound asleep. However, my mother continued to listen attentively as I explained. She occasionally stopped me to ask a question. The notion of the support of Kielian snakes staggered her.

"Snakes? I hope you're joking! They have no native intelligence. They're lazy —"

"They've never been challenged, Mum. We don't know what they might be capable of. Please hear me out." I paused. I knew what I was going to say next was going to be difficult. "Mum, when our pine tree was hit by those hireclaws, you could have lost me, as well. It was Gilda who saved me. She couldn't save Lysa or Gundesfyrr, but she saved me."

Mum's eye teared up. I extended my wing tip and stroked her back feathers. "She found me, Mum, and she dragged me to safety. Kielians are very strong."

"I know," she replied in a small voice. "At least, that's what they say. But what exactly are you getting at, Lyze? Because, although they may have many good attributes, they aren't owls. They can't fly."

"I'm not worried about that now," I said.

"I'm so relieved," Mum said, somewhat sarcastically. Her tone didn't bother me in the least. I was delighted to see that I had genuinely engaged her in this conversation. She seemed to be emerging just a bit from her fog of grief.

I closed my eyes for a moment and drew in my mind a picture of a fleet, a light-armored unit. A striker unit! That's what it would be. Because we would strike before a conflict could even begin. We would complete daring midair reloads, and Kielian snakes would serve as nimble ground forces. The notion of a few — for a few was all it would take — Kielian snakes smashing a repository of ice weapons to smithereens was riveting. Bylyric might be a tyrant. He was brutal. He fought savagely, but not with his head. We would bring a new kind of war to the Orphan Maker.

CHAPTER 20

For a Kingdom?

"Look, look at them, Mum! It's almost like they're flying!" Ifghar hooted as we caught our first glimpse of the Hock.

Indeed it was. The sky seemed to sizzle on this nearly moonless night with iridescent jolts of light as dozens upon dozens of Kielian snakes leaped from the cliff. It would be impossible to pick Hoke out from the hundreds of snakes that shimmered in the night air. But that was not what occupied me at the moment. I was studying their descent as they plunged. Some floated down slowly, others fell at a blistering speed toward the churning waters beneath them. They evidently had ways of controlling their speed. How could this be? They had none of the arsenal of feathers we had to shape the wind beneath our wings. They couldn't shift spoiler flaps into gear, as we could, to slow for landing. What could they do, for they were just long vertical, wingless, legless, slithering tubes covered in scales? Their shape alone defied such possibilities.

"Slow down and enjoy it, Yentse!" someone hissed. I believe it was a cerulean lazuli but I couldn't be sure. I watched the snake carefully.

"Didn't your mum ever tell you not to stare?" she hissed at me as she drifted through the air in a slow dive.

"Oh, sorry. I was just so fascinated at how you can adjust the speed of your descent."

This seemed to please her.

"Well, glad you appreciate it! My son down there doesn't get at all the finer points of diving yet. It's all just a quick plunge for him. Look at the pretty designs we can make!" With that, she curled herself into a tangled triple loop and scrolled the night with shimmering hues of blue against the blackness. For a moment, it was as if she were nearly still, as if she had stopped the world for a long, languorous hover. I noticed a collarlike ruff of scales that had extended from her neck. It wasn't dissimilar from the secondary set of scales that I noticed on Hoke when he had smashed the rock so long ago.

"You see," she said as she coiled herself into a double helix. "We can lighten our bodies."

"How do you do that?"

"Hordo knows!" she said. "It's connected with breathing and then these." The scales on her ruff shimmered as she fanned them out, and her speed slowed. *Are they like wings?* I wondered. This was all enormously fascinating to me.

The snake's name was Dylan. She invited my mum, Ifghar, and me to her nost.

"Where's the young'un we saw diving with you?" Mum asked.

"Hordo knows!"

"Who's Hordo?" Ifghar asked. I was mortified by this question, but Dylan shrugged it off.

"Hordo, dear," my mother said, "is the Kielian snake spirit. We have Glaux, our spirit. They have Hordo."

"But ours is better, right?"

Mum and I both gasped. I was horrified. But Mum replied sweetly, "Ifghar, there's no such thing as a 'better spirit.' It's not a competition."

A croaking sound issued from Dylan's throat, the sound of Kielian snake laughter. "Oh, goodness, you owls are so curious. What would you like to know, young'un?" she said to me.

"Lots, ma'am," I said.

Ifghar cocked his head. Mercifully, he remained silent, but I saw the question in his eyes. *She's a snake — why did you call her "ma'am" like she's important?* The words might as well have been spoken, and I saw a glare rise up in Dylan's slitted eyes.

"First of all, what species of Kielian are you?" I asked.

"I'm not a nest-maid," she replied sharply, and then, as if to put a finer point on it, she showed a bit of fang. "There has never been a nest-maid in our family. I am a cerulean lazuli with a touch of cobalt." As she said the word "cobalt," a silvery blue seemed to flash through her scales. "The cobalt is mostly visible on bright sunny days or under a full-shine moon."

A torrent of questions poured from me — how long could a snake hold its breath underwater? What were those scales that flared like a ruff to slow her plunge?

"My extended scale plates, or ESPs,[24] as we call them."

We talked for several minutes before my mum said, "Lyze, don't you think you've asked enough questions? We don't want to wear our host out."

"Just one more question!"

"Go ahead, young'un," Dylan said.

"All right. I know you've never served as a nest-maid, but have you ever thought of another kind of service?"

"For owls?" she asked. Her eyes slitted, revealing only a glowing line of luminous cobalt.

"For the kingdom," I replied quietly.

---

24 Extended scale plates (ESPs) are one of the most intriguing structures of a Kielian snake's anatomy. They are not only connected with the snake's ability to adjust its descent when diving from a high cliff, but also intricately involved with the muscles and nerves that control the head's shaping mechanisms.

CHAPTER 21

General Andricus Speaks

On my first day back on Dark Fowl, I found myself in General Andricus Tyto Alba's hollow with his topmost advisors explaining my ideas for a "newfangled" fighting force.

"The unit would be very small compared to most commando units," I explained.

"How small is small?" the general asked.

"A dozen, no more."

"A dozen!" Captain Nillja Micrathene Whitneyi exclaimed. She was an Elf Owl who had distinguished herself in the Frost Beaks' unit as a superb strategist.

"Yes, Captain." They were all looking at me very skeptically, except for the general. They would only be more incredulous when I revealed my plans for Kielian snakes. I thought I might as well get that over with quickly.

"Small, but a mix of species," I added.

The owls in attendance all blinked. There were derisive snorts and hisses.

"Let him finish," General Andricus shushed them with a wave of his port wing.

"I propose using Kielian snakes, mostly as ground troops." This wasn't entirely accurate, but I didn't want to startle them with the idea of snakes in flight on the backs of owls. There was complete and utter silence, but the air reeked with contempt.

"And I suppose he has a role for, let us guess — white-footed mice?" an ancient Barred Owl muttered under his breath. I knew this was my biggest problem — getting these owls to begin to think of Kielian snakes as actual soldiers and not just mindless rock crunchers or honers. I stole a glance at the general. He seemed lost in deep thought, his white, heart-shaped face as blank as a pale winter sky. When at last he swiveled his head toward me, there was a shimmer in his black eyes that snuffed out the din of scornful whispers.

"And have you thought of what such a unit might be called?"

I felt a calm creep through my gizzard, which had been fraught with tension. *He's with me,* I thought. *The general is with me.* And a name came to me, I'm not sure from where. I took a step closer to him and spoke up in a strong voice. "The Glauxspeed unit, sir."

His black eyes brightened. "And a fine name it is. Glauxspeed! What do you say to a division?"

Everyone gasped. General Andricus swiveled his head to fix each owl in the small assemblage with his fierce, dark gaze. "A division composed of several of these hyper-maneuverable units. Together, we would call them the Glauxspeed Division."

"B-b-but, sir —" Captain Nillja began to sputter.

"He's just a young'un!" a Barred Owl interrupted. "He doesn't even graduate until, when?"

"Soffen issen," I said softly. I was completely confused. Certainly, General Andricus was not suggesting that I command a division?

He must have read my mind, for he turned to me and said, "Listen to me, Lyze of Kiel." I started, as did everyone else, for he did not address me as Cadet Lyze Megascops. This was an egregious departure from protocol. I was almost dizzy now with confusion. I felt all eyes settling upon me in anticipation of what General Andricus was about to say. "I am not suggesting that you lead this division at all. You don't have the experience in the field — yet. But you have an idea. You picture all this in your mind's eye, do you not, lad?"

"Yes, sir, I suppose I do."

"You flew out and rescued Orf. A small unit of mixed species rescued the best blacksmith in the Northern Kingdoms."

The general lofted himself onto a higher perch and paused until a hush enveloped the hollow. It was so quiet that as I watched a plummel fall from the cantankerous Barred Owl, I swore I could hear it touch the floor.

"You see, my friends," the general continued in a gentler tone, "we're at a critical juncture in the war. The war is changing and it's coming closer to home. I have just been informed of three more attacks on peaceful communities." He paused again.

"I cannot make this clear enough." His voice swelled. "We are losing! As of this moment, the Ice Talons League has gained more territory than they have lost to us. By soffen issen, our slipgizzles tell us the front will be here — here, at Dark Fowl Island! Bylyric is planning a massive invasion, and he and his forces will fly on west and south. Yes, it's true. They've set their sights on the Southern Kingdoms. On Ga'Hoole!"

I felt a darkness fill my gizzard. It began to twist and twitch. The Elf Owl Captain Nillja staggered on her tiny feet.

"Ga'Hoole!" someone whispered.

General Andricus flipped his head. "The great tree itself. And we're all that stands between them," he said quietly. "Cadet Lyze has seen over the murky horizon, a horizon stained by the blood and smoke of old methods of combat. We need new, young flexible minds quick with imagination to invent new strategies if we are to have any chance. And that is exactly what Cadet Lyze, Cadet Loki, Cadet Lil, Cadet Blix, Cadet Moss, and the master's apprentice Cadet Thora can offer. The success of this division depends not simply on training, however, but on secrecy and surprise. I cannot emphasize that enough. Secrecy and surprise! The Ice Talons must never know what's coming if we're to retain any advantage."

"So you are elevating these young cadets to the rank of division and battery officers?" a Spotted Owl asked with more than a tinge of contempt.

"No. Not now, Major Fina Strix Occidentalis. But soon. For now they shall become instructors in this new form of fighting. We need to have this division ready by spring. We must be able to meet Bylyric's invasion with hidden strength. Bylyric plans to be here, here where I perch." His eyes bore into the Spotted Owl. *Let that sink in*, he seemed to be saying. *Imagine a tyrant on this perch.*

"Lyze," he said, "tonight a new cadet arrives, a certain Cadet Strumajen Strix."

"The daughter of Commander Strix Hurth who used to teach here?" someone asked.

"The very same."

"But she was a terrible problem to her parents, disobedient, disinterested in her studies. Dis — dis —" the Spotted Owl began to sputter.

"And now distinguished," General Andricus said coldly, leveling those impossible dark eyes that looked like dead coals in his white face. "Yes, Major Fina Strix Occidentalis, she was not fit for entry into the Academy here. She had to go to the second-rate school — Gareth's Keep, up by Little Hoole. But two evenings ago, we received a falcon messenger with the news that an earthquake in the region had destroyed the remaining walls of the fortress there, making Little Hoole vulnerable. Wave upon wave of Ice Talon units stormed the breach. Apparently, under the most unimaginably terrible conditions, this young owl, whom everyone had always thought was a huge disappointment . . ." The general lingered on the last word so that the sound of it seemed to sizzle through the chamber. "She drove them off. This cadet acquitted herself with unmatched courage and, when forced into a seemingly untenable position, managed to fend off a much larger enemy force. She will be invaluable to the formation of the Glauxspeed Division." And then under his breath, perhaps so as not to offend the older owls who were gathered in this hollow, he muttered, "We need bold, new owls, with bold, new ideas."

Glauxspeed Division! The words rang in my ears and rattled my gizzard. I was still dizzy from all the general had said.

I was not to be an officer, at least not yet. But I was to be an instructor — this seemed to me an even more daunting promotion. How did one transform oneself from student to teacher that quickly? By soffen issen, that was the deadline. For that was when the fight would arrive here — here at Dark Fowl Island.

The image of Lysa as a small, dark lump on the snow came back to me in all its horror. The soot on her tawny new feathers seemed to stain the whole world. The rumors about Bylyric abounded. Some said he was part hagsfield, that beneath the white plumage of a Snowy, there were the dark feathers of the ancient hag owls who had practiced nachtmagen in the time of the legends. If that was so, what good would my newfangled ideas and strategies do? My strategies were based on logic, developing a keen sense of the weather, advances in weapons, and most of all, faith in ordinary creatures being trained to do extraordinary things. And faith was not magic.

The idea of a small unit had been tested in a limited way when we rescued Orf. But "limited" was the key word here. There had been six of us. Now we were talking about an entire division made up of many smaller units, each very specialized in a new way, yet able to work together when needed.

Loki, Blix, Moss, Lil, and I — the five of us together must show the others.

CHAPTER 22

Strumajen Strix

If I had pictured a romantic reunion with Lil, I was to be disappointed. When I found her in the eastern barracks where the female cadets were billeted, she was in a small hollow with none other than the distinguished Cadet Strumajen Strix. They were in the thick of a conversation about battle strategy. Lil looked up at me with her bright, gleaming amber eyes and my gizzard twitched. "I was just telling Strix Struma — she likes to be called that — about the rescue of Orf, and our ideas."

The Spotted Owl looked at me, nodded her head very respectfully, and said in a quiet voice, "Brilliant. Just brilliant! If I'd had a mid-flight reload during the attack on Gareth's Keep . . . what I could have accomplished."

"I understand that you did plenty as it was," I replied. Strix Struma was much younger than I expected, younger than Lil or me. Obviously, she was some sort of child prodigy, and I liked her immediately. There was a keenness in her gaze, and I liked the set of her feathers.

"So how did it go with the general?" Lil added. "Moss

caught me up on things and told me you were with him to discuss a new unit."

"Well, yes . . . uh, the good news is the general really likes my ideas. And we have a name for it. There's just one little problem. It's not exactly a unit, Lil. It's a division. The Glauxspeed Division."

Soon, we were making a list.

"All right," Strix Struma said. "In the Kielian League, a division is made up of three to five hundred owls. So we begin with that."

"Owls," I said rather vaguely. "That's a bit limiting."

"What do you mean, Lyze?" Lil asked. Strix Struma looked slightly confused as well.

"What about snakes?"

"Snakes?" they both uttered. Bewilderment clouded their eyes.

"Yes, Kielian snakes." I began to explain my thoughts about snakes and how they were underutilized.

"I like it," Strix Struma said slowly. "I like it a lot."

"I love it!" Lil explained. "Ground troops would certainly give us an edge."

"And that gives me an idea," Strix Struma said. "Let's think of other animals that could help us."

"Polar bears," I said. "But they sleep most of the winter so they'd only be available to serve during soffen issen at the earliest and then through ny schnee."

Something flashed through my mind. The mangled talon of Hrenna, Moss's mother. I turned to Lil and Strix Struma. "Moss's mother! She leads a commando unit called the Flying Leopards." It was so still, I could have heard a plummel drop. "Supposing," I continued, "there were other ground troops linked with the Kielian snakes — a unit of snow leopards."

"They're pure muscle," Strix Struma said. "There were several around Little Hoole. They can climb anything — sheer ice cliffs. Their paws are huge. I saw one once knock a polar bear senseless. And they can swim."

We began scratching madly on a birch bark. Moss arrived and we worked through twixt time and on past noon, never taking a break. By First Lavender, we had a rough organization for the Glauxspeed. We had reworked the standard size of a division and its normal subunits. While standard military division sizes were anywhere from three hundred to five hundred owls, our division was a scant three hundred forty animals, composed of two regiments of one hundred owls of mixed species, fifty Kielian snakes, and twenty snow leopards. The division was further broken down into battalions composed of twenty owls, ten snakes, and ten snow leopards each.

Finally, there were the smallest units made up of twelve owls, five snakes, and five leopards each. The unit was what I had first envisioned — a combat group that was light, fast, and flexible, both in the air and on the ground.[25] And could shatter the very gizzard of the Orphan Maker!

---

25 The organization of owl military divisions has always differed greatly from those of the Others. After extensive research in many of the volumes of the Others' military history, I found that a division was composed of between ten thousand to twenty thousand soldiers with at least three brigades.

CHAPTER 23

Glaux + Speed = ?

"All right now!" Dylan snapped at the snaggle[26] of the dozen snakes that coiled before her. "I want to see those ESPs go to full extension. Cadet Jena, I wasn't born yesterday. I might not be a striated violusian, but I've been diving with them for longer than you can remember. You can do twice what you're doing now. You want to fly?"

"Yes, ma'am —"

Dylan reared up into a high, tight coil and hissed, showing a lot of fang.

"I mean, yes, Master Sergeant Dylan Lazuli!"

"Well, you ain't getting off the ground at this rate. No owl will want to carry you. The more you spread your ESPs, the lighter you will become to help your owl get airborne."[27]

---

26 A "snaggle" is a Kielian snake term for a group of snakes numbering between six and twelve.

27 If the reader would like to learn more of my theories on owl-snake flight dynamics, I suggest he or she read the volume I coauthored with Hoke and Dylan: *A Brief Analysis of the Dynamics of Kielian Snake-Owl Flight.*

I watched these exercises every evening at First Lavender, even when I wasn't part of them. When the more advanced snake students were ready to embark on their first flight, Lil and I, along with Loki and a half-dozen other owls, became their vehicles. In the beginning, we owls were a bit nervous because the snakes were a new kind of weight. We had to learn how to balance ourselves and trim our wings to fit the burden. It was especially challenging when snakes went from a recumbent position to a full or half coil for strike. Their center of gravity shifted and could send us spinning. But once we learned how to cooperate, the rewards were bountiful. When the snakes expanded their ESPs, it could provide fantastic lift. In an odd way, it was similar to soaring, but there were no warm thermals involved.

"All right now, troops, we'll make two passes with all cadet snakes in position number one. On the third pass, assume a half coil and a double-blade ax-head shape. Fourth pass, coil to full position, maintaining the double blade, and extend your scale plates. Owls, you'll feel a slight lift. And remember, owls, the snakes are your copilots. If you need more lift, just say 'full extension.'"

The progress the newly recruited snakes made was amazing. Their head transitions were smooth, they coiled up on the backs of the owls in flight, and they hardly ever wavered. We knew that snakes would be invaluable on the ground, but we hadn't been sure how they would do in flight. But they were learning fast. On another part of the field, more advanced snakes were engaging in target practice. Owls flew above snakes, with dummies suspended from their talons. The snakes took aim and struck like lightning.

We were also making great advancements with midair reloads. Great Grays and Snowies worked particularly well as reloaders as they were the most deft in sidling up to the tiny owls that composed the Frost Beaks. But we were also now training Eagle Owls and Barn Owls as reloaders for larger weapons. Thora's quivers were proving quite revolutionary, and we knew they would prove invaluable in combat. Then Loki came up with the brilliant idea of not just reloading with weapons but refueling with food in noncombat situations, such as reconnaissance missions. The small owls, like Elf, Pygmy, and Northern Saw-whets, who were most often used for reconnaissance, burned up their energy sources faster than larger owls. They got hungrier quicker and fatigue set in. But if a Snowy or Great Gray could carry prey, just a tiny snow mouse or a rockmunk, the smaller owls wouldn't have to stop to hunt.

To build a division with creatures ranging from owls to snakes and — we hoped — snow leopards was not easy. One of the first things that I insisted on after I located Dylan, Hoke, and

Gilda was that snakes be given official ranks as members of the Kielian League. The first started as master sergeants.

Then we began the snake recruitment process in earnest. It might seem counterintuitive, but I purposely looked for the laziest snakes I could find, the snakes who were distracted in the honing pits, or the excavators who were bored with knocking their heads against rock barracks. I sensed that these snakes were intelligent but had never been truly challenged.

My theory was simple but it worked! The nest-maids who were completely stupefied from slurping up vermin in owl hollows flocked to our recruitment stations. We instilled in them a sense of pride.

Those first few weeks passed so fast. General Andricus might have appointed Moss, Lil, Loki, Blix, and me instructors, but we were learning as much as we were teaching. The second week, Moss was dispatched to fly to the far north where the snow leopards lived on the ice cliffs above the H'rathghar glacier. In addition to recruiting snow leopards, he was also charged with recruiting more large and powerful owls — Eagle Owls, Northern Hawk Owls if possible, Great Horneds, and Great Grays.

Almost nightly, Peregrine Falcons flew in with postings from the front. We would watch them land and race immediately to General Andricus' headquarters. The tension in the air was so thick you could cut it with an ice scimitar. A weird silence fell over the entire island each time a messenger landed. The only sound heard was the rasp of the Kielian snakes in the honing pits.

Bad news seeped out in bits and pieces from command headquarters. The front was moving closer. A colonel had been wounded, a celebrated general killed, and worst of all, another peaceful community razed and hundreds of owlets left orphaned or dead. Every day, new troops mustered on the flight parade grounds of Dark Fowl to go to the front and support the tactical squadrons engaged in combat. My mother had been called back to her unit and resumed her position as a commando with the Ice Daggers. Word had come in to me that a broody had been installed for my brother, Ifghar, who was proving to be a talonful.

In the third week of training, an especially fast peregrine, Glynnis, flew in at a truly amazing speed as I perched at the top of a silver fir tree where I had been observing midflight reload exercises. I feared the worst when I saw how fast she was flying. What was it? Had disaster wiped out an entire brigade? It was as if the sky, the very clouds, parted for her.

When I realized that she was flying directly to the crown of the silver fir where I perched, my first thought was that something had happened to Mum. I began to wilf.

"It's good news!" Glynnis announced. "At least, I think it is. I can't read code."

"What?"

"News from Moss," she replied, handing me a white bark with a message written in Hollow Code:

⊣⌐ ⊃⌐ ⌐⌐⌐⌐⊃∨⌐⊣∨⌐∨⊣⊏∨

It read: "Have recruited six snows." I knew at once he was speaking of snow leopards. This was extraordinary news. It was all coming together. For the first time, I had real hopes of our being ready by the spring offensive.

We needed more snakes — as many as possible, and especially the really large ones. Gilda had told me there were some very large fellows at the eastern end of Stormfast. I had wanted to go check in on my little brother, Ifghar, and I thought I could scout for a few large snakes at the same time. So I went. Little did I dream that what I found on that scouting trip would have such an immense impact on the rest of my life.

Dear reader, might you guess of whom I write? Her blue-green scales are glittering now as she makes her way into my hollow while I write these words. She is bringing me my dawn constitutional — a cup of milkberry tea laced with a dram of bingle juice. I must go back and cross out the words "blue-green." She would be furious at my lack of precision in calling her blue-green, or Glaux forbid, bluish or greenish. How well I remember her first words to me. . . .

CHAPTER 24

I Meet Octavia

She was large. She was lazy. Her parents had given up on her, but she had a prodigious intelligence. And she would become my best friend throughout the many long years that were to follow.

I had been flying over a slot in the cliffs where the sea broke in when I spotted a large — forgive me once more — bluish-green snake. She was reclining on a rock, hardly stirring. Indeed, I overheard her ask a blind nest-made snake to fetch her a minnow the next time it dove into the sea. *The nerve!* I thought. *Why doesn't she get it herself?*

Suddenly, I remembered that Dylan had told me about an enormous and enormously lazy snake who looked just like this one. Dylan had met her mum and da once when she had worked for a spell in the honing pits. They had complained about their shiftless daughter, a problem snake and silly as a rockmunk. When she wasn't lazing about, she was off flirting with fellows. I circled her three times with growing excitement before I alighted on a rock nearby.

"Hrrh, hrrh!" I cleared my throat in an attempt to rouse her. Nothing. I coughed a bit louder and saw her eyelid flicker. "Pardon me," I said. "I could not help but notice how handsome you are." Her other eyelid flickered now — I was getting someplace. "I've never met a greenish-blue snake before."

At that, she exploded from her relaxed position and coiled up, hissing like nothing I'd ever heard.

"And you're not now!"

"Huh?"

"You're not meeting a greenish-blue snake, you poop-brained idiot! And what's this 'ish' business? Sloppy language! Greenish-blue! Outrageous! An offense to my species, my class. Numbskull!"

"What are you, then?" I asked.

"Let's start with what I'm not! I'm not a cyan verdigris, but a cyan celadon."[28]

"Oh! I'm so sorry. For a snake of your beauty, your absolute pulchritude, I can imagine the offense." I was really laying it on thick. I could tell I was dealing with a snake who wasn't just lazy, but vain, too. I was willing to do almost anything to get her in the division. I sensed potential. Glaux knows how, but I

---

28 Octavia tells this story in a slightly different way. She claims that I went to her parents and said something to the effect that I promised that if they gave her to me, she would never have another lazy day in her life. She also leaves out the part of how she insulted me.

did. If Moss could recruit snow leopards who spoke in a strange dialect that owls only half understood, I should be able to recruit this one snake.

"Pulchritude?" she asked, a question in her voice. Perhaps she had never heard this word for beauty, or was impressed that I had. I pushed on. "There is a grandeur to you. An elegance enhanced by your size, and I suppose that is what first attracted me —"

The momentary flash of confusion in her eyes stopped me. "Are you trying to woo me, owl?" she said warily. Her eyelids closed, showing just glittering slit of green.

"No, I was actually attracted to you for quite other reasons." Now I clamped my beak shut. *Let her wonder!* Silence filled the air, and her scales began to twitch with curiosity.

"Well?" she said.

"Well, what?" I replied with a half yawn.

"Are you going to tell me what compelled you to light down and insult me with that 'ish' word?"

I was playing her now. And rather enjoying it, I might add.

"A terrible breach of conduct on my part. Please forgive me."

Her eyes closed until I could see only a hint of sparkling cyan, like the tracery of a distant shooting star. "Listen, buster, I don't give a white splat of seagull poop about apologies. Tell me why you decided to set yourself down here!"

I leaned in. "This is top secret. You must not breathe a word to a soul."

"Agreed," she said curtly.

"I have been charged by General Andricus Tyto Alba to form a new division for the war. We are recruiting the best of the best, not just owls, but snow leopards."

"Snow leopards!"

"Yes and —" I paused a few seconds. "Kielian snakes."

"Kielian snakes! How will they serve?"

"Some as ground troops, some in the air."

"In the air! How?" she demanded.

"They'll fly on the top of owls," I answered. "We have a training program going on now on Dark Fowl."

"No!" she gasped.

"Yes." I could see I was beginning to reel her in. "We'll set some snakes down in enemy territory. We especially want to use them for espionage."

"Espionage." The word slithered off her forked tongue.

"Exactly. And beautiful snakes will be better able to insinuate themselves into situations than unattractive snakes. But I also need snakes that are large and strong."

"I can bust rocks like nobody's business, fella."

"My name is Lyze by the way. Lyze of Kiel."

"Well, Lyze of Kiel, sign me up!" The snake paused and then uncoiled herself to lie flat, not for rest, but in a gesture of submission. "I am Octavia, your humble servant, willing to follow you into battle."

I cannot describe how touched I was by her words, her gesture. And she has been my humble servant through war and peace, through death and despair, through solemnity and joy. She kept me going when I thought there was not another wing beat in me. And, I might add, she never had another lazy day in her life.

CHAPTER 25

Octavia Flies

Octavia began her training that very night. "Teach me! Teach me now!"

"Teach you what?"

"To fly! To fly on your back."

"B-b-but, Octavia, first you have to get to Dark Fowl! It's not a long swim. The currents this time of year will carry you there swiftly."

"It's not as fast as flying," she said, slyly narrowing her eyes. "You can teach me."

"I've never taught a snake! Other Kielian snakes teach the snake recruits."

"But you've certainly carried snakes during their training, or how could they learn? Come on, let's try it," she said, and there was something so persuasive in her voice that I couldn't resist.

You have to remember that a Whiskered Screech is definitely a midsized owl, perhaps even at the smaller end of the midsized range. We are three times the size of a Northern

Saw-whet or a Pygmy or Elf, but far from the huge dimensions of a Great Gray or an Eagle Owl. I staggered a bit when Octavia, who was no sylph, crawled onto my back.

"Get used to it. Get used to it," she said gently. "Walk around a bit." I'm not a Burrowing Owl, who are known for their ability to walk, run, and even dig earth with their strong legs, and the thought of stomping around with a load of snake on my back wasn't especially appealing. So I did not walk far. In fact, I took only two steps before I turned directly into the wind.

"Why are you turning this way?" Octavia asked.

"Your first lesson: I am calculating the headwind and crosswind. Owls always take off into the wind."

"Why?"

"Because a headwind generates more lift. I want you to partially engage your ESPs for takeoff. This will accelerate our climb."

I heard the whisper of Octavia's extension scale plates as they began to unfurl. It was incredible! I lifted off in half the time it normally took carrying a snake, and Octavia was the largest snake I'd ever transported. She began instinctively to do the special breathing that Kielians had mastered for swimming underwater. The breathing inflated her pulmonary air sacs and, by some strange alchemy, made her lighter in the air.

"Great Hordox!" Octavia exclaimed. "I — I — I can't believe it. I'm almost at a loss for words!" I had a sense that this rarely happened to Octavia. But then I caught sight of her shadow printed against the moon as she reared in a spiral on my back. Together we made a fantastical two-headed creature of wings and helical twists soaring through the night.

"This is the most wondrous thing! I — I — I'm rapturous!" she cried, and the words rang out into the sky.

Never had a snake aided an owl so superbly in flight. To see her unfurl those immense scales that collared Octavia's neck stirred my gizzard. She was intuitive about the winds.

To fly well, one must deploy all the natural devices that we owls possess. There are the principal flight controls — our wings that flap up and down and propel us forward. Then there are the smaller, secondary movements of our wings that shape our feathers to take fullest advantage of the wind. Through these minuscule adjustments, we can avoid wild yaws and pitches from unexpected gusts that sweep in sideways and throw us off balance. Now with the Kielian snakes' ESPs, especially Octavia's, it was as if we had gained a third set of controls that revolutionized combat flight. Soon you could hear owls shouting, "Bless Hordo!" or Kielian snakes crying out, "Bless Glaux!" during difficult maneuvers.

Within three days of our return, Octavia had been promoted to the rank of master sergeant and served along-side Hoke, Gilda, and Dylan, instructing other Kielian snakes on "bi-flight," the term we settled on for aerial combat using snakes and owls. The first time I heard an owl say, "Bless Hordo!" my gizzard quivered with joy. For I knew my idea for the Glauxspeed Division was truly working — an assortment of different species was coming together in a combat unit.

And it was none too soon. The news from the front became grimmer every day. There were now so many orphaned owls that refugee camps had been set up for them. If Bylyric invaded, who would take care of the young ones? Would they be raised under the tyranny of that evil owl? What kind of world would that make?

Lil and I were spending a great deal of time together, both while we trained and off the training field. We were frightened to talk about a future — with the war growing hotter, it seemed like tempting fate. We lived from night to night, and after all the drills and strategy sessions, as the blackness began to thin into the pale pink of dawn, Lil and I would meet and fly off as far as we could get from the Academy. If the temperature was right, we played scooter scooch, sliding down the winds toward the sea, our shadows dancing on the sun-splashed water. But the best times were when we found a little patch somewhere and talked, telling each other of home and our hollows. We tried not to think of war.

I told her about my strange tantya Hanja, who always appeared on the brink of impending disaster. Lil churred when I told her these family stories. I loved the sound of Lil's laughter. It was so rich and lilting, like a song in itself. But I wondered if we would ever have new family stories to tell.

Every day brought us closer to the season of soffen issen. The slightest change in temperature rattled my gizzard. I had vivid daymares of melting ice and the issen blomen, the ice flowers that sprouted in spring at the edges of glaciers and avalanches. In my dreams, the issen blomen melted into pools of blood, soaking through snow scattered with broken and singed feathers.

Late one morning when Lil and I returned, Blix and Loki were waiting for us. They were so excited they were almost jumping out of their feathers.

"He said yes!" Loki clamored.

"The general said yes!" Blix snapped her beak and twittered, a common vocalization for excited Saw-whets.

Loki explained, "General Andricus has consented to your request to go to Shagdah Snurl to do —"

"To do all that stuff!" Blix broke in with a clacking of her tiny beak. "You know, the weather stuff, all that scientific stuff you're always talking about. And the best part is we get to go with you! We'll be your guides."

I swiveled my head toward Lil. This was a wish come true, but sometimes the best wishes . . . well, they come with shadows.

"Lyze," Lil said, touching my chest with her wing tip. "It's wonderful! You might discover things that could really help us."

"Lil, the general says that you're to take over the Kielian snake training, along with Octavia, of course," Loki said.

"I am!!" Lil's luminous eyes shined with pride.

The orders to go to the Shagdah Snurl made perfect sense. Preparations for the Glauxspeed Division were well under way, and it had been reported that the Ice Talon forces were totally occupied with preparations for the invasion.

"But we can't deceive ourselves, Lyze," the general said in my meeting with him. "They're going to come back with a vengeance. We've been busy working on our new strategies with the snakes. They're going to be planning their own new tactics."

"Do you think they know about the snakes, sir?"

"I hope not. We've had surveillance owls out constantly,

and you know we've shut down the grog trees on this end of the island. It's a no-fly zone. But you never can tell. So get some rest. I want you to depart at First Lavender with Blix and Loki for Shagdah."

"Yes, sir."

I was about to leave the chamber when the general called me back. "Lyze, I nearly forgot."

"Forgot what, sir?"

"I just got a message from your mum. Your younger brother will be coming here for his first cadet moons. He'll arrive before you return. Your late father was one of the bravest owls I knew, and your mother is a superb commando in the Ice Dagger unit, not to mention your truly inventive military mind. I'm sure Ifghar will make us all very proud."

I felt a slight twinge in my gizzard and almost said, *I hope so.* But I caught myself and nodded my head crisply. "I'm sure he will, sir."

"Dismissed."

I knew I had to rest, but I was so excited I could hardly sleep. It would be difficult not seeing Lil, but she was so supportive. She kept repeating how this trip was a chance of a lifetime for me. Before I left, we went out to our favorite place at the end of the island and soared on the thermals over the sea. The moon was rising full and golden, casting a wide, glittering path of light across the dark sea. We flew close to each other, our wing tips often touching and sometimes our wings overlapping, printing one immense wing against the sea. It was almost as if, in those moments, we became one owl, for I could not see where I left off and Lil began.

"Lyze," she said. "You might learn something on this trip to end the war! And then . . ."

"It's almost unimaginable, a world without war," I said.

"But that's exactly why this trip is so important." She extended her wing tip to touch my flight feathers, and I felt a pulse streak through me. I was suddenly too shy to look her in the eye and studied the water beneath me.

"Lil?" I whispered.

"We could become wingfast." Once more our wings slipped over each other.

I swiveled my head toward her, my eyes filled with disbelief. "What?" I whispered. "Say it again!"

"Wingfast . . . you and me."

She believed in me. She believed in me so much that she dared speak of a future. I couldn't help it; it made me cry. She gently lifted a wing and dried my eyes with the soft feathers of her plummels.

"Someday, Lyze, when there's no war, we'll discover old and wonderful things together."

My gizzard now was absolutely tingling. A future . . . a future with Lil! The love of my life. The love of my future. For I had the peculiar feeling that we had always been together in some way. That we were two old souls who had finally come together again on the far edge of an endless, tired war.

CHAPTER 26

Virtual Light and True Black

The Shagdah Snurl and what I thought of as its core, the Nacht Sted, were known as the hatching place of the winds. But I knew we weren't flying toward a nest tucked up with rabbit's ear moss. It would be hard to imagine a plump broody clucking encouragingly in this desolate stretch of land. No, instead, it felt as if we were flying toward a boiling cauldron presided over by one of the legendary hagsfiends from the past, with wings dripping ragged black feathers.

None of these notions seemed to afflict Blix or Loki. The Shagdah was home, sweet home for them! My first task was to disentangle myth and legend from truth and reality. The flight required two whole nights, taking us so far north that the sun barely rose. We were going from night to night, so to speak, with only the smallest splinter of light to crack twixt from tween time. Blix and Loki knew instinctively what time it was, without needing the sun as a marker. And these two owls, the Great Gray and the Northern Saw-whet, could fly rambunctious winds the likes of which I'd never seen before.

I had just recovered from a hard bounce off the leading edge of a rogue airfoil. "Great Glaux!" I exclaimed. "These are real Snurls, aren't they?"

"Sorry, Lyze, but they're not," Loki replied, rolling easily off a similar foil. "These are just the pre-Snurls."

"Watch me," said Blix. "I am going for the top of that airfoil you see curling above that cloud. You see those threads of turbulence on its lower edge?" Owls can't see wind precisely, but we can feel the threads of it brushing our filoplumes, as we call those very fine feathers on our faces. "Well," continued Blix, "we call those threads baggywrinkles. Watch me climb them and catch a ride on the crest of that airfoil."

The tiny owl did a sort of scooter scooch up through the baggywrinkles and zipped through the air above the foil. The way she moved was what inspired my studies of airfoil structure."[27]

Soon I saw Loki go into a steep, banking turn. I guessed we were approaching his hollow, although there were almost no trees in this region, save for the occasional thin patch of northern birch. The owls of the Shag, as the natives called it, lived in ice-clad lava cliffs.

---

27 *Wind Dynamics: An Exploration of the Shape and Structure of Airfoils.* This is a slender volume I wrote, which involved a fascinating experiment where I "inked" the skies by dropping plumes dipped in ink into a variety of foil formations and, with the help of my colleagues at the Glauxian Brothers retreat, recorded patterns key to a foil's structure.

A low pitch warbled across a vast field of jagged dark rocks tipped in ice. "Whooooo . . . Whoooo . . ." It was the unmistakable call of a Great Gray. "Loki!"

"Mum!" Loki whoooed back.

A Great Gray flew out of a cleft in the cliff to greet us. One of her wings was bent, which gave an odd slant to her flight. "Dear lad! My dear, dear lad!" she cried. "And darling Blix!" Introductions were made and we were led into Wynnifryd's hollow. A kinder, lovelier Great Gray I have never met.

"I just put a naked rockmunk on the coals for myself," she said. "But, Loki dear, why don't you go out and fetch some more? There's a mess of them scrambling around on the rock where you used to take off to play scooter scooch."

"Naked rockmunk!" I repeated. "I never heard of such a thing."

"They're native to the Shag, Lyze. New tastes here, you know." This was quite the understatement. I had never tasted cooked meat before. When Loki returned with three more of the rockmunks, Wynnifryd slapped them on a bed of coals from the shores of the lava lake.[30]

---

30 When I arrived at the Great Ga'Hoole Tree many years later, I was the one who introduced cooked meats to the tree. Up until that time, fire and coals were only used for blacksmithing. When I became head of the weather-interpretation chaw, however, I insisted that all food be consumed raw when on weather missions. It was difficult to interpret weather with a bellyful of warm meat. It threw off one's senses for such analysis.

"You didn't by any chance see a peregrine, darling, did you?" she asked.

"No, Mum. Why would there be a peregrine around here?"

"My question exactly. This is the most unpopulated place on Earth, especially lately."

"Yes," I replied. "The front has moved far from here."

"I don't go out much, you know," she said. "Lots of my old friends have died. There are still a few families around with young'uns serving. Probably grandchildren if anything. We are not a young crowd up here." She paused. "We're not a crowd at all. That's why I like it!" she added brightly.

Loki's mum had been injured, and her mate killed in the Battle of Firthgot. For a time after, she served as a quartermaster in charge of weapons inventory and delivery systems to the field. She was especially interested in our ideas for midair reloads.

"I am so, so proud of you, lad!" she said, her voice breaking. "Oh, Loki! The major would have been so proud of you had he lived."

The naked rockmunks were simply delicious, so succulent. They were called "naked" because they had no fur whatsoever. They didn't need it, because they lived in the warm tunnels on the rim of the lava lake.

We stayed with Loki's mum for a few days and I explored a variety of steam vents, smee holes, and layers of thermal air around the area. It was as if the landscape was constantly shrouded in sea smoke, except there was no sea around. The whole landscape was covered in rock that had melted eons ago and solidified.

As fascinated as I was by the Shag, I really wanted to get to the Nacht Sted, the coldest and most desolate place on Earth. There was a volcano with a lava lake there surrounded by several ice caves, and these caves fascinated me the most. This was the safe season to visit, according to Blix and Loki, because the volcano was quiet and not hurling lava bombs into the sky.

I was terribly excited as we approached the Nacht Sted. We flew over a long-dormant volcano, its crater like a charred crown rimmed in silver frost. I could feel an acute drop in temperature.

I wanted to know how ice could form so close to fire. Would this ice have special qualities that we could use in some way? I dreamed of an entire new arsenal of equipment that we might unleash on Bylyric.

The winds were ferocious, and the ice that fringed the cave entrances was scalloped by the constant onslaught from these gusts.

"Wind sculpting," Blix explained. When I looked across the top of the craters, I could spy the northernmost reaches of the Bitter Sea, a cold, cold sea choked with ice.

"We want to show you something before you start your studies," Blix said in a somewhat ominous voice.

"Are you sure, Blix?" Loki asked. There was a flash of apprehension in his yellow eyes.

I was immediately burning to see what Blix wanted to show me. Burning, that is, as much as one could burn in a place like this.

"It's going to give you the creelies," Loki warned. "I mean, you're going to wilf. The first time I saw it, well, I wilfed so much that I was almost as small as Blix."

"Just take me there!" I screeched in frustration, though it was hard to screech above the wind.

"All right, all right already!" Loki said, and spread his wings.

We entered an ice cave on the north side of the extinct volcano. The opening was not much more than a slot, and Loki had to tilt his immense wings at a sharp angle to pass through.

"This slot wasn't always here," Loki said.

"It opened up the summer before we went to the Academy," Blix explained. "It was even smaller then. It was a really tight fit for Loki."

Aha! I thought, remembering how bashed Loki's wing tips had been when I first met him, and his lame excuse about molting.

"Follow me," Blix said. "I know the way."

We followed a long, winding tunnel, flying in some places and walking when the ceilings got too low. The slot began to enlarge eventually, and we came into a spacious cavern. The air was very still and we couldn't even hear the wind howling outside. There was barely any light. I was so curious, I could almost feel my pupils enlarging.[31] Then I saw it. Something white hanging from a spike of ice in the distance.

"What is it?" I whispered.

"A face," Loki said, his voice trembling.

"A face of what?"

"Of an Other . . ."

My heart skipped a beat. This truly was the place where myth and legend collided.

---

[31] Owl eyes are not spherical in shape like most creatures but are elongated tubes. Owls have large pupils that collect all available light, giving us excellent eyesight in the dark.

CHAPTER 27

Myth Meets Truth

"Look at his feathers," Blix said as we inched closer.

"Feathers but no wings!" Loki whispered.

"I don't think those are feathers," I said.

"What are they?"

"I'm not sure," I replied, peering at the strange creature. "How did he get here?" I asked. "You said the slot just opened before you went to the Academy."

"There's a crevasse at the very top. We hadn't noticed it when we used to fly up here, because it's iced over. This Other must have fallen through long, long ago."

The Other was the most peculiar creature I had ever seen. No myth could have been stranger than the truth that confronted me. I poked gently at the body. It swayed slightly. It was definitely not clad in feathers. Its covering was made from some kind of woven material, like so many of the relics discovered in the ruins of Others in the Southern Kingdoms. A peculiar contraption was attached to his back, almost like a very large botkin a blacksmith might carry. Metal objects that looked like gizzard rippers hung from the creature's sides. They roused my curiosity. I hovered in the air, examining them more closely, then swiveled my head toward Loki and Blix.

"I don't like the idea of filching from the dead, but I think we must take some of these metal objects."[32]

"But is it dead?" Loki asked.

"It's dead all right," I replied.

"We thought . . ." Blix seemed to hesitate. She began again. "We thought at first maybe it was a frozen scroom."

"A scroom? A ghost? No!" I said. "Not at all. This is too . . . too real to be a scroom."

"Scrooms are sort of real," Blix muttered.

I had never seen a scroom, but I had heard enough about them. Scrooms were the restless souls of owls that roamed the Earth because they had unfinished business and could not yet leave for glaumora, the owl heaven. I pecked slightly at the creature again. It was dead.

On his head, it wore a strange thing that looked somewhat like the helmets favored by warrior owls of Ga'Hoole, but it wasn't made of metal. Some of the same color fur that grew on his face also blushed out from beneath his helmet, only much thicker.

---

32 In addition to the metal spikes, there were also metal loops. I would later learn that the spikes were called pitons and designed to dig into rock cracks, and the loops were called carabiners and used to link systems of rope in a sport the Others called "mountain climbing."

I thought about what Blix had just said — how scrooms were sort of real. I turned to look at the tiny owl. "Yes, scrooms are sort of real. I won't deny that such things exist, but I feel they exist because of our memories. We have no memories of this creature, so it cannot be a scroom."

I was not sure if what I said was true, but it felt true to me. I realize that this is a peculiar comment from an owl like myself, who purports to be a scientist and relies on data, testing, and experimentation.

I pecked at the creature again. "You can't peck at a scroom," I said. "It would simply dissolve."

This Other wasn't dissolving. Far from it. Indeed, I began to wonder if the reason it was so well-preserved had something to do with the frigid temperatures and dry air of the Nacht Sted.

For the next several hours, the three of us worked on picking loose the metal spikes and the loops that hung from his side. Loki and Blix agreed with me that it was important for Orf and Thora to take a careful look at these. We didn't think they were weapons, but perhaps we could adapt them in some way for combat.

"Can you fly with that, Blix?" I said, looking at her as she took off from a ledge with a loop in her talons.

"It's heavy, but if I can balance it just right, I think I can," she said.

We were most interested in the spike. On further examination of the Other's botkin, we discovered a quiverlike object into which the spike fit.

"Interesting," Loki said as he shoved a spike into the quiver. I heard a tiny click as if something had engaged. Suddenly, there was a load crack and a flame shot from the quiver, the spike whizzing by Blix and missing her by a sliver. It stuck in the wall of ice, still burning.

"Holy Glaux!" she exclaimed, staggering in the air with the loop still clutched in her talons. "That wasn't a quiver — it's a launcher!"

"A fire launcher!" Loki said. "This is far more dangerous, far more powerful than fire claws, and it doesn't damage our talons. This is the weapon of the future!"

I was still dazed by what we'd seen. My eyes fastened on that flame that was still burning in the ice wall. How had the spike been ignited in the first place? I recalled the click I had heard just before the loud crack. Had there been a little spark then? Was there some sort of fuel in the launcher? I remembered the sap in the pine that had caused the tree to explode the night Lysa died.

Before we left, I wanted to examine our weapon. Carefully, I laid out the spike and the quiver in which it fit. The click I had heard came from a tiny mechanism with interlocking teeth like bits on a small disk. I began to move the disk with my talon.

"Be careful!" Loki said.

"Don't worry, it's not loaded now. It won't do anything." I could see that the secret to its power was a spring that doubled the speed of the thrust. On further examination, I saw that the spike itself had notches interlocked with the launcher. It was a devilishly clever invention.

We knew we had a dangerous item in our talons, but we were determined to take it back to Dark Fowl and show Orf and Thora. We found a second launcher in the botkin and decided we would take two launchers, several spikes, and one metal loop. We would have to fly with the utmost care.

We vowed to come back to the ice cave in the Nacht Sted, but for now we knew we must leave. We had discovered more than we had ever expected, but I still wanted to learn more about the place where the winds were hatched, where the jealous sisters Snurla and Solskynn clashed in the dim mists.

"Imagine if Snurla and Solskynn had got hold of these spikes," Loki mused. "There might not have been a myth after all. They would have killed each other instantly."

"Exactly," I said. But I felt my gizzard wrench. These might not have been weapons for the Others, but for us owls, they could be incredibly deadly. I was almost exultant at the thought that this could end the war once and for all. I began to imagine a life with Lil, a peaceful life. Wingfast! We could be wingfast and all because of these fire spikes!

CHAPTER 28

Half Beak and Three Talons

We emerged from the ice tunnel into the harsh light of the Nacht Sted ice field glaring under a full-shine moon. The long shadows of the four-legged creatures slanted across the ice, and the wings of a Snowy threw great shadows against the silver disk of the moon.

"Good Glaux!" Blix cried. "Moss!"

This was Moss's secret training ground. Of course! What could be more secret than this desolate place? Had General Andricus known this when he granted my request to visit? I doubted it. Moss had been charged with finding a secret place, not ordered to go to one already specified.

It was mesmerizing to watch the big cats stalk across the ice. Their walk was a silken motion, sinuous and silent. I couldn't hear their paws touch the ground; they were as silent in their stride as owls are in flight. Beneath their marbled pelts lurked an unimaginable power. Their long tails swayed back and forth languorously, but I dreaded what the lash of their tails could do. Yes, these creatures were built to kill.

"Look, he's found his big owls, too," Loki whispered. "Two Great Grays and two Great Horneds and an Eagle Owl." Moss hadn't mentioned finding any owls in his coded messages. We had worried that his outpost was too remote, and we couldn't recruit.

We were about to call out to Moss when Blix noticed something. "How bizarre!" she said. "One of the Great Horneds is missing half a beak."

My parents' words from an evening long, long ago came back to me: *We left our mark, didn't we, Sweet Gizz? Darned hootin'! Your da raked off half the Great Horned's beak, and I snapped off not one, but two, of the other fellow's talons.*

The owls that had mutilated and nearly killed my mother were there in the moonlight, helping Moss train the snow leopards!

"Half Beak!" Moss cried out from the distance. "Guide them from the rear into the first defense configuration."

"Wait!" I hissed at Blix. "Don't say a word." The Great Horned was a slipgizzle. Moss must have inadvertently recruited slipgizzles! I wilfed to half my normal size, and both Blix and Loki looked at me in alarm.

"Whatever is it?" Blix said in a tiny whisper. Her words fell as quiet as snowflakes.

"That's the owl that attacked my mum!" My voice was trembling. "And that one flying just above the lead snow leopard's head, that's another one!" For indeed, the other owl was missing talons. "They're slipgizzles working for the Ice Talons."

"What?" Loki and Blix looked at me, stunned.

"Slipgizzles!" I repeated. "Think about it. It would be easy for an owl to slip in around here, pass themselves off as wounded hireclaws, not able to go into the field but ready to help in training. Moss was up against time. He didn't have the luxury to check out every owl."

"What are we going to do?" Blix asked.

I flapped my wings in agitation. "I'm not sure. They're big, powerful owls, and all we have going for us is surprise."

I saw Loki glance down at the launcher in his talons, and my gizzard twisted.

Suddenly, an idea came to me. *Code!* Moss was a master of all the Kielian League codes. He was especially good with the hardest of them all — the spoken code.

Our plan was a simple one. Blix was to do the speaking while Loki and I sequestered ourselves behind a large, ice-sheathed boulder.

We held our breath as Blix flew out.

"Blix!" Moss cried out.

"Verschtucken mitgon vouykinn schnitzkin bynnghis yonkus!" cried Blix. The spoken code is Krakish, but with double-meaning words. What Blix said in Krakish was "Hello, rockmunks are among us. My friends, the two Horneds." But it meant: "Beware, slipgizzles are among us. The enemies, the two Horneds."

From our vantage point, we could see that Moss was about to wilf, but he fought it hard. The two Great Grays were looking stunned, as well the Eagle Owl. They obviously understood the coded language, but the two Great Horned Owls did not, nor did the snow leopards. Except for this first small slip, Moss was doing a fantastic job of concealing his shock. The Snowy, my friend from earliest childhood, stayed as cool as any battle veteran.

In the spoken code, Blix told Moss where we were hiding. We could not hear the entire conversation for the wind was up again, drowning out many of the words. But it appeared that Moss called a halt to training for the night, though dawn — or the virtual dawn — was still some hours away, and then set up a guard rotation for the night.

"It's all right," Loki whispered to me. "We outnumber them."

"They're twice our size! And they could call in other owls, other enemy troops. There could be other Ice Talon owls holed up all over this place. Remember that peregrine your mum mentioned flying around? We could be outnumbered."

From our sequestered perch, we could see that every creature, both owls and snow leopards, were extremely nervous that evening and ready for anything but sleep. Blix pretended to sleep in a small notch in some rocks. As dawn neared, I spied Half Beak rouse himself, swivel his head about slowly as if checking that his companions were asleep, and loft into flight. He flew straight out toward the Bitter Sea, quite far out, and when he returned, he wasn't alone.

CHAPTER 29

Spikes in the Night

At least eight owls and a peregrine stormed out of the darkness. The snow leopards leaped into the air, their huge paws striking the night. A Hawk Owl plunged down in a kill spiral for Blix, but went kerplonken when it saw a snow leopard take to the air in a huge jump. The leopard missed its target, but the owl crashed into the ground and broke its neck.

The night turned into a maelstrom of violence. Feathers and blood swirled in the mounting wind gusts.

"Lyze!" cried Loki. "The launcher!" He was loading up a spike.

There was a strange spitting sound as it whizzed across the field. An owl plummeted to the ground, a burning spike in its breast. Loki let out a warrior's whoop and immediately began to reload. A Hawk Owl was brought down by one of our Great Grays, but an enemy Eagle Owl was coming in fast on Moss, and Moss was already showing a streak of blood on his coverts. *His blood or the enemy's?* I didn't have time to think. I raised my launcher, and a spike sliced the night. The next thing I knew, the Eagle Owl, the largest of all owls, plunged through the sky and fell dead to the ground, a spike thrusting from his chest. I reloaded and shot again, another spike slicing through the air. A scream tore the night, so piercing and unearthly I thought the moon would crack and the stars would fall from the sky. I couldn't see who I'd hit.

In only a matter of seconds, the skirmish was over. It had only lasted as long as the silver flash of a moonbeam darting through a cloud. I suppose you could say we'd won, but it didn't feel like a victory. Moss, Blix, Loki, and I swept over the battle-field to see the fallen. One of our Great Grays was dead, and a snow leopard named Patches was severely wounded. A spike was hanging from her haunch and burning off her fur, the spike I had misfired. It was the snow leopard who'd screamed in that terrible, haunting way.

Moss swooped down, yanked the flaming spike from the leopard, and hurled it into a snowbank.

Blix had done training as a field medic, and she and Loki tried to stanch the bleeding.

I made my way over to the peregrine, who was still alive but not for long.

"Glynnis!" I whispered, shocked. "I — I thought you were on our side."

She was gasping for breath. Blood gurgled from her beak. "You thought wrong, dearie!"

Never had a term of endearment sounded so nasty, the word a vicious sting in the night. "Your little secret is out," she gasped.

"What little secret?"

"The snakes! The snow leop —" But the words died on her beak.

What General Andricus had said came rushing back to me: *The success of this division depends not simply on training, however, but on secrecy and surprise. I cannot emphasize that enough. Secrecy and surprise!* My gizzard collapsed within me. Everything was for naught. All the training, all the inventions, the new ideas — for naught! Bylyric knew all our secret strategies. The Orphan Maker was going to win.

While Blix and the others tended to the wounded, I went around the battlefield and retrieved every single fire spike. I flew directly out over the Bitter Sea and dropped them into the churning waters, along with the two launchers that Loki and I used. They were too dangerous. I felt in my gizzard that they were the first step to total annihilation. As the churlish seas parted to welcome the last spike, I wondered if this was why the Others had vanished. Had they fallen in love with weapons and assured their own destruction?

I did not know. I am more of a scientist than a philosopher, and just then, my mind was clouded with thoughts of the invasion to come.

CHAPTER 30

Wingfast

When I got back to Dark Fowl, I found Lil on an empty training field practicing with Miss Hot Point. She was concentrating so hard that she didn't see me at first. When I churred at her, she dropped her lance and wheeled around, streaking toward me. We wrapped our wings around each other as we slowly alighted on the ground. I emitted the mellow, warbling trill, and Lil replied with a low, whinnying call. For the first time, we dared to sing the prelude of the courtship song.

Yes, we were ready to become wingfast and, within hours of my return, the bryll branch had been fetched, for that was the traditional perch for a couple getting wed. We asked to have the ceremony in General Andricus' hollow at headquarters. There was a crack in the hollow that was normally plugged with ice and rock, but the general cleared it carefully so we could see the Light Bringer, the morning star.

I had fetched Octavia, Blix, and Loki, and Lil had found Thora and Orf. The only missing owls were Strix Struma and my brother, Ifghar. I found Strix Struma perched on the very top of a silver fir, taking in the view of the training field. Her attention was focused on my brother.

"There you are!" I said. "I've been looking all over. For Ifghar, too — I'm so excited!"

"Oh, Lyze!" she said. "I'm happy you're back safe and sound. About Ifghar — that snake friend of his —"

"Not now! As a matter of fact I have to fly down there and fetch —"

"Lyze!" she interrupted firmly. "It's about Ifghar and his training. We should split up your brother and that snake Gragg."

I frowned at her. This was my wingfast day, and I didn't want to be bothered with minor training problems.

"Fine!" I said. "Split them up. But now, please let me talk! I'm here to invite you to Lil and my wingfast ceremony!"

Strix Struma blinked. "That's wonderful." She gave Ifghar a nervous glance. I could tell that there was something disturbing her, but I didn't have time to worry about it then. It was my wingfast day!

Lil and I took our places on the bryll branch. Thora had found some ice flowers and made a garland for Lil that draped down from the crown of her head to her lovely tawny shoulders. The tiniest issen blossoms and astrilla blume fell around her like a cascade of pale pink stars. Her talons were bare — neither of us wore battle claws. I realized it was the first time in forever that I'd seen her talons. She had cleaned them with balsam fronds, and they glistened pearly white.

Just before the final guest arrived, I heard a scuffle outside the hollow. After talking to Strix Struma, I'd been late, so I'd asked one of the general's aides to fetch my brother. It became obvious that he wasn't aware of the nature of the occasion. I could hear his voice rising in anger outside the hollow.

"Well, Sergeant Luka Strix Varia, I do not see why Cadet Gragg, who is training with the Glauxspeed Division as a second-degree Kielian copilot, cannot be included in this meeting with the general. We are both exactly the same rank as cadets and —"

"I have my orders, Cadet Ifghar Megascops," said the sergeant.

"Your orders!" grumbled Ifghar.

Strix Struma's voice broke in crisply. "None of that, Ifghar! And don't hiss at me, Gragg! I'm your commanding officer."

"Thank you, madame," said the sergeant.

"Is Lil here already?" Struma asked.

"Yes," the sergeant replied, a slight smile in his voice. "She's inside."

"It's a veritable party," sneered Gragg.

"It is a party, of sorts," said Strix Struma. "It's a wing-fast ceremony."

"A wingfast ceremony?" I could hear Ifghar gulp. "Whose?"

"Who do you think?" I heard the sergeant say. "Your brother and Lil."

Ifghar looked numb as he entered the hollow. Except for one odd, almost stricken glance at Lil, his eyes were as hard as stones. But I didn't let it distract me. This was our day, mine and Lil's. The light of the morning star poured down through the crack in the hollow and wrapped us in its soft glow.

General Andricus Tyto Alba began to speak. "Cadets, officers of the Kielian League, blacksmiths — friends of Lyze and Lil, we gather here at twixt time under the Light Bringer to sanctify and bless the union of these two owls, Major General Lyze Megascops Trichopsis, commander of the Glauxspeed Division, and Battalion Commander Lillium Megascops Trichopsis." He turned to me. "Under the wings of Glaux and the eyes of the stars, do you, Lyze, take Lillium . . ."

THE WAR MOONS

CHAPTER 31

For Shame!

Your little secret is out.

The words of the treacherous Peregrine Falcon Glynnis haunted me in my waking hours as well as in my dreams. The slipgizzles at the Nacht Sted had robbed us of any chance at secrecy and surprise, and it was difficult for me to tell General Andricus the devastating news.

"To what extent did she betray our strategy, Lyze?" the general asked.

"We can't be sure," I answered.

"We have to assume the worst." He paused, deep in thought. "Which means we need a new surprise, a new strategy."

I looked at him blankly. *Like what?* I wanted to ask, but I resisted.

"Where are Moss and the snow leopards now?"

"They've moved to a new black site to complete their training."

"Well, good! That's a start. And how is their training going?"

"They're a strong team." I didn't want to think of the snow leopard Patches, stabbed in the haunch by one of my fire spikes.

"Look, Lyze, we have to go with what we've got. A strong team now finishing their training in an undisclosed location." He paused. "We're scant moons from what is supposed to be the start of the invasion."

"I know," I said softly. I was sick with worry and, for the life of me, I couldn't comprehend why the general seemed almost jovial.

"Furthermore, rumors are flying that Bylyric is beginning to move his troops into position."

"I've heard," I said.

"But there have been no sightings of Bylyric himself."

"Oh."

"Oh, you say. That's interesting, isn't it?"

"Yes, it is," I said, but I struggled to understand why.

"I wager he's still holed up somewhere in the Ice Talons." The general's black eyes glinted meaningfully at me.

"Sir, what exactly are you driving at?"

"Surprise, Major General Lyze Megascops! Surprise. We invade them! You and your Glauxspeed unit go straight for Bylyric! Take him out, and his whole army collapses."

My beak dropped open.

"Don't you see it, lad? This is the perfect situation. Now's the time." And as he explained, I began to see his peculiar logic.

As the nights grew warmer, the hard ice began to soften. We owls are creatures of the north. We love the cold and the sparkling clear skies of deep winter, when the constellations burn their brightest. We even like the shrieking winds and the stinging sheets of snow, but winter is not the best time for combat. The same brightness of air that reveals the stars lays bare our troops. The long, never-ending nights we love in peace can cause an owl at war to lose track of time and fight beyond his natural endurance. No, spring and summer are the war months. The skies roil with thick, oily clouds perfect for camouflaged flights or what we called HALO, or High Altitude Low Opening operations.

Snowies and Great Grays are perfect for HALO ops. They blend in seamlessly with the cloud cover and can hover down and drop in Kielian snake ground troops or slipgizzles. This was how we planned to discover the whereabouts of Bylyric.

We doubled our training. The division was coming together, and Ifghar was doing much better. He had changed after we separated him from Gragg. As soon as we put them in different units, Ifghar seemed to develop a better attitude. He adapted to a new snake and made new friends in his unit. Some, I must admit, were more impressive than others. It disturbed me slightly that he was drawn to owls who seemed to me easily influenced. His companions didn't quite have a sense of service to a greater goal. I was concerned, but I had a lot on my mind with the spring offensive a few short moons away.

There is really never any quiet time on Dark Fowl Island. Toward the end of the night, troops began to fly in from the forward operating bases, and the din is unbelievable. For myself, when the evening training sessions finished, there were always strategy sessions and weapons reviews.

One evening, just as the last real darkness began to shred before the dawn, I was making my way over to visit Cronin, the quartermaster. Thora and I had planned to meet there to look over weapons that might need refitting before spring. I paused for a moment by a grog tree where a certain old Snowy, a very popular fellow known as the "blink skog of Dark Fowl," was telling an old story about the myschgrad serpent, a legendary snake who lived at the bottom of the sea. It was said that when the serpent twitched, the earth convulsed, and fire sprang from the depths of the sea. I only meant to stay for a minute — I had no need of tales of twitching serpents, not when I knew Bylyric and his troops would soon be bearing down upon us. But there was something so mesmerizing about the way the blind skog told this tale, and I had been hoping that Ifghar would show up.

I hardly ever had time to talk to him these days, and sometimes I wondered if he was avoiding me. Our exchanges on the training field were almost perfunctory. I knew he was deeply proud of the special battle claws I had Orf make for him when he first arrived, but he had never thanked me for them.

When Ifghar didn't appear, I lofted myself into the air. My business at the quartermaster's hollow didn't take long, and once Thora and I finished reviewing the various flails, billy hooks, and hot blades, I proposed we go by the grog tree again to see if we could catch Ifghar. On the way, we heard a scuffle that appeared to be coming from a stand of birch trees.

"Someone's crying or — or mewling," Thora said.

I heard it, too, and voices as well. We made a tight banking turn and headed for the stand of trees, alighting very quietly in the top of the tallest birch. I wilfed when I recognized the taunting voice of my brother, my baby brother! He had his talon crunched down on the port wing of a small Sooty Owl called Cadet Gabi Tyto-Ten.

"Forgot your claws, Gabi?" Ifghar sneered. "And why ya got that Sooty face? Not a true Barn Owl?"

"Got a hagsfiend for a mum?" asked a Spotted Owl.

The other cadets laughed, but the worst laugh of all came from Gragg, who curled up on Gabi's other wing and raised up his cudgel-shaped head to slam it down with a sickening crunch. Thora let loose with loud screeches and swooped down on the bullies.

I took a mighty swipe at Gragg's sensitive mid region and immediately his head snapped back into its normal shape. "Didn't know I knew that trick,[33] did you, you half-wit?" I yelled.

Thora ripped off Ifghar's battle claws.

"You can't do that. Those are mine!" Ifghar howled.

---

33 This "trick" was something that Hoke had taught me. Many snakes, particularly in their immature years, can't maintain head shape if struck in the midsection of their bodies. Thank Glaux it worked.

"Oh, yes, she can!" I thundered at him. Cadet Gabi Tyto-Ten had a broken rachis, the central shaft in one of her primaries, and she was bleeding from a torn calamus.[34] The wound was not irreparable, but Cadet Gabi wouldn't be flight ready for some time. This was beyond rhotgort, a small rule infraction. This was actually vroknenplonk — an offense that could get all of them de-commed.

The bullies wilfed down to half their size. Gragg's once-fat head was now the size of a bingle berry.

I fixed my gaze on each one of them for several seconds, but saved most of my fury for Ifghar. "This is not the matter of a rhotgort," I said.

"Yeah, yeah, sure —" Ifghar began to talk nervously. "I mean, take away my battle claws for a while. I've learned my lesson."

"Shut up, Ifghar," I roared. "This is not a matter of a rhotgort because you have injured a cadet. Cadet Gabi Tyto-Ten will not be able to fly. You have committed the gravest of offenses. For shame, Ifghar. For shame on all of you!" I was trembling with anger.

"It was just a joke, for Glaux's sake," Ifghar protested. There was a desperate note in his voice that made him sound as if he were fighting for breath. It had no effect on me.

---

34 The calamus is the hollow feather shaft that attaches to the skin of a bird.

"It wasn't a joke!" I stormed. "You are all of you bullies and you have committed a treasonous act. This is a matter for vroknenplonk."

The young owls gasped.

Three nights later the Vroknen, the high military court, found Ifghar, Gragg, and their two owl friends guilty of treason. They were given dishonorable discharges, except for Ifghar, who was spared because his mother and father had both served so long and illustriously as officers of the Kielian League. He was permitted to plead guilty to the lesser crime of conduct unbecoming to a cadet. Ifghar was put in the brig for the remainder of his training and would only be allowed to serve in noncombat situations. His battle claws, as the custom decreed, were melted down.

"We'll use the metal for a pellet pot," Thora sneered. Owls in the brig were not permitted to go outside to yarp pellets. When the call of nature came, they were reduced to yarping in a pot.

CHAPTER 32

"The Price We Pay! The Price of War!"

A few weeks after Ifghar's trial, General Andricus sent me away with Loki to deliver a message to one of his lieutenants. Normally, he would have used a messenger falcon, but he understood I needed to get away from the Academy. Ifghar's behavior had left me badly shaken.

The mission took us over one of the Kielian League's refugee camps. Hundreds of owls had been left hollow-less or orphaned in recent moons. Often their parents were off fighting and their caregivers — their broodies or elderly aunts and uncles — had lost their lives. The attack that Moss and I had endured on Stormfast had been unusual at the time, but the Ice Talon League had begun attacking peaceful communities as a regular war tactic. This particular refugee camp was at the southern edge of the H'rathghar glacier.

We are prone to think of glaciers as endless expanses of featureless ice. But as the glaciers approach lower altitudes, small forests can spring up along their edges. This settlement camp, called Lav Issen, which means "low ice" in Krakish, was full of young owls. As we flew over the camp, we saw that all the available hollows were crammed, and owls were even huddling in old, rotten stumps. A small contingent of Kielian snakes was working its way through the camp, pulverizing the centers of stumps to create makeshift nests, and another group of owls and snakes were dragging in rotten logs to be used as well.

No sooner had we alighted than I caught sight of the soft purple hues of a striated violusian.

"Gilda!" I exclaimed. She had just slammed her head into a tree stump, and she blinked when she heard her name.

"Lyze! Dear Lyze! And Loki!" She coiled up, tears glittered in her violet eyes. "Oh, my goodness! You're here!"

She slithered over to me and began to loop herself loosely around my shoulders.

"You aren't out flying with . . . with . . ." I momentarily forgot the name of the Snowy she copiloted for.

"Jonor," she said. "He died. He took a fizgig to the skull in a skirmish off the Firth."

My gizzard seized. "How did you survive?"

"I fell into the ocean, and remember, we can swim."

"So what are you doing here?"

"Waiting for my next assignment. I didn't want to just coil up and do nothing. They need all the help they can get in these camps. Look around you at all these orphans. This is the price we pay! The price of war!"

She paused. "You know, dear lad, I was never the best nest-maid snake. I wasn't particularly good at keeping hollow, but I do rather enjoy smashing things up." She whacked the rotten stump and peered into the cavity she had formed. "This is a nice cozy space — big enough for at least four Pygmies and a couple of Elf Owls. I left a bit of an overhang so the black-smiths can make a metal piece to serve as a roof."

"Very nice, Gilda," Loki said.

We hadn't flown far when Loki cried out.

"Mum!"

"Loki!"

I couldn't believe it. There was Wynnifryd, tending a fire with three voles roasting on it.

"Mum, what are you doing here?" Loki and Wynnifryd wrapped their huge wings around each other, their faces radiating pure joy.

"What am I doing here, son? My bit. My bit."

"But your wing?"

"I can fly — a tad cattywampus, but I got here," she churred.

"B-b-but — what are you doing here?"

"What does it look like? I'm taking care of these young'uns and introducing them to the delights of cooked food." When we perched on the log, I hadn't noticed half a dozen little owlets upwind of her. She turned to them now.

"All right, little ones. Want to sing the song I taught you?"

"Yes, Wynnie!" they cried.

She took up the forked twig with which she had been turning the voles.

"Now, a-one and a-two and a-three . . ." Six little peeping voices began to sing:

> There're voles in holes
> And voles on coals.
> Yummy, yummy in my tummy!
> All so nice and warm,
> Warms you once,
> Warms you twice.
> Roasted voles
> Are awfully nice.

"Nicely done! Now eat your voles while I take our visitors around the camp."

Wynnifryd took us on a tour. The first thing I noticed was the unnatural silence that enveloped the camp. Normally, when a bunch of owlets get together, there's a constant racket of noisy chatter — gazooling, the elders call it. And owlets are always playing.

No one was playing here. Very few were even flying. It was obvious that many had been orphaned before they had fledged, and there weren't enough adults to begin them on branching. Many of the owlets looked so thin and tattered that I had to wonder if they'd even have the strength to branch. The fledged owlets had feathers that were so sticky with burrs and debris, it was doubtful they'd ever felt the gentle preening strokes of a cleaning beak.

A little Spotted Owl who had just begun to budge was perched on a stump, crying. A Snowy tried to comfort him.

"I know I'm not your mum. But I can keep you warm, and why not try to eat this bit of mouse? I took the fur off for you. Come on now, take a little bite."

"But I'm not hungry!"

Wynnifryd leaned over and whispered in my ear. "Some of them are too weak to eat. That's why I cook their food. It's easier to get down." She turned to Loki. "Fly back to my griddle and get that last vole. We'll bring it to this little one and try him on it."

It was heartbreaking. Later that same afternoon at tweener, we perched in a large hollow with Wynnifryd and the camp director, a Lieutenant Lyngaard Strix Varia.

"We're not as flooded with orphans as some of the other camps. It's tragic," he said. I could not help but remember the dreadful night when Lysa died. If she had lived, would she be in a camp like this? Would I have ever been able to find her?

The lieutenant swiveled his head toward me.

"I suppose you have heard, Lyze, that your brother has been recommissioned?"

"What?" I was stunned. "So soon? Why?"

"We desperately need soldiers. I hate to say it, but we can't be picky. No offense."

"None taken. My brother has been the offense. I hope he redeems himself on the battlefield."

"May Glaux guide him."

CHAPTER 33

Into the Ice Talons

It was not long after we returned from Lav Issen that we dispatched our first contingent of Kielian snakes to spy in the region of the Ice Talons. Lil, Strix Struma, and I, along with three others, conveyed the snakes to the drop point. Octavia was commander of the operation on the ground.

We flew in under the thick cover of an early morning fog — the perfect conditions for a drop. There was a long, quiet moment as we said good-bye on a wind-bashed, sea-scoured rock a few leagues west of the Ice Talons. I peered into Octavia's glittering green eyes, but I couldn't glean what she was thinking.

She was setting out on an unbelievably dangerous mission. She and four other snakes were going to penetrate the labyrinthine network of ice passages behind the three peninsulas that spread like icy talons across the thrashing waters of the Everwinter Sea. Collectively, these fingers of ice were known as the Ice Massif. If she or any of the snakes were caught, they would be executed immediately.

Octavia had become my closet friend and confidante other than Lil, and I shared worries with her that I dared not share with Lil. The Kielian snake and I spoke no words in parting. We nodded to each other and then she was gone, slithering through the crashing waves as she made her way toward the southernmost prong of the ice formation.

I perched on the rock and followed Octavia with my eyes as long as I could before I lost sight of her. It was as if a part of me went with her. I caught myself holding my breath each time she dove under the water, and peered hard to make out her head — just a dark dot in a cresting wave — when she surfaced.

She later told me the incredible story of her mission, which I now transcribe here in her own words.

I could feel Lyze's bright yellow eyes following me as I swam. I knew he dared not fly over me in case the fog thinned and he was spotted by enemy scouts. We both knew that we might never see each other again. But if I died on this mission, I would die happy. Lyze had given me a life, and I didn't need death to understand that. I knew everything had changed the first moment we met. A lazy, selfish, and very unhappy snake had been offered a matchless opportunity — a chance for a meaningful life of dignity, service, and grace.

It did not matter to me that I was a snake fighting for owls. In a world on the brink of disaster, what difference did it make which species one belonged to? Lyze an avian, myself a reptile — we were all in this together against the most terrible tyrant the Northern Kingdoms had ever known. Differences are muted under these circumstances.

Nevertheless, I was terribly afraid. This mission was very dangerous and I'd heard horrific stories about what the enemy did to slipgizzles. Bylyric had black sites not for training, but for torture. Many of them were rumored to be deep in the Ice Talons — secret chambers where unimaginable atrocities were performed.

The current was with me. As I swam, I rehearsed my cover story. I was coming back home, home from the Southern Kingdoms. I had served down there as a nest-maid snake in the Great Ga'Hoole Tree but — and this was key — the southern owls preferred the snakes native to the great tree. Those snakes were blind, and everyone knew that the owls of the great tree were very secretive.

If it were true that Bylyric had his eyes set on the Southern Kingdoms, he would take this bait. What better source of information on the Southern Kingdoms than a nest-maid snake who had served at the great tree? They would be fascinated at what I had seen while I was there.

In preparation for this mission, Lyze and I had pored over every document in the military library that related to the Great Ga'Hoole Tree. I could name every snake guild of the great tree, from that of the harp guild to the weavers and the lace makers. The Plonk family singers' papers were also in this library, and Thora, a descendent from that line of distinguished warblers, had told me everything her family knew about the great tree. I was ready.

The three other snakes that accompanied me were not to penetrate into the labyrinth as far as I was. They were to lie low around the outer perimeters doing what carefree Kielian snakes do best — diving and having fun. At this season, snakes often took annual diving trips to the Ice Narrows. If I found out something critical, the three other snakes would serve as my transmission agents.

It didn't take me long to begin my work. I lingered briefly around the southernmost talon when a smallish Spotted Owl approached me.

"What are you doing here, snake?" His amber eyes bore into me. "Been diving in the Ice Narrows?"

"No, I'm anxious to get home. But the wind and current are against me."

He was very still and kept staring at me. It was unnerving, like he was sizing me up. I felt I had suddenly become completely transparent, and he would be able to detect every lie I was about to tell.

"Get home from where?" he finally asked after what seemed like endless minutes of silence.

I tried to steady my voice as I spoke, but at the same time, I looked around for a quick escape. All I could think about were those black sites where slipgizzles were tortured. "Southern Kingdoms," I said as casually as I could. "I've been down there for a spell."

"That so?" His eyes flashed as he blinked, and he tapped his battle claws on the ice.

"Yes, but I live way up the Firth of Fangs and I need a job."

"You don't like lazing about like most of these snakes?" Once again he tapped his battle claws, and then he dragged them a bit across the ice. The sound shivered up my spine.

"No, I don't, actually. I like fishing — fishing for capelin." I knew that on the Ice Talons, where red meat was scarce, the owls mostly ate fish. But Fish Owls as a species had proven loyal to the Kielian League. For fishing, the Ice Talon owls had to depend on Eagle Owls, who were not nearly as good with small fish like capelin.

"We might be able to use you in low mess," he suggested.

I felt a quiver pass through my scales. This confirmed that there was an Ice Talon contingent still embedded in the southern talon. And if there was a low mess, there might be a high mess hollow for high-ranking officers.

"Follow this lead." He flipped his head toward the narrow

channel on the north side of the southern talon. "You'll see a Burrowing Owl there. Tell her Wick sent you for service in low mess."

I did as I was told and soon encountered a Burrowing Owl who was furiously digging out a small ice hollow, or schneddenfyrr, the kind of nests that birds of the nearly treeless north often built for their eggs. I had not seen one of these in a long time.

"About to lay an egg, madame, I presume?"

"Here? Are you yoickers?" the Burrowing Owl snapped. "Don't presume anything, snake. I'm done raising chicks. I'm making this for myself. We're running out of space inside the Ice Talons." She clamped her beak shut when she realized she'd said too much. "I mean, I prefer to have a hollow that opens directly on the lead. The ice here is easier to dig." Her featherless legs began whacking at the ice.

"Let me help you with that." In one swift stroke of my head, I doubled the volume of the schneddenfyrr.

"Oh, my goodness!" the Burrowing Owl exclaimed in delight. A small stream of ice worms tumbled out at the same time.

"Not to worry," I said cheerfully. "I do worms as well." And I quickly slurped them up.

"Oh, you are a wonder! The ice worms and the frost vermin are real pests around here." She flipped her head about and then upside down as she surveyed the ice walls and ceilings that tunneled through the Talons. "The whole place could use a good cleaning up." She swiveled her head sharply and looked at me with narrowed eyes.

"What brings you here?" It was as if suddenly she felt she had let her guard down and become too hospitable, too intimate. Her eyes hardened with suspicion.

"Wick directed me to you. He thought I might serve in low mess. You know, providing capelin."

"And you fish, too!" A brightness was rising in her eyes, the anticipation of something delicious, luscious. But she quickly quenched it. Once again I had caught her off guard. Desire, craving had no place in the Ice Talons, for it was equated with weakness. She squared her shoulders and in a curt, no-nonsense voice said, "Follow me. I'll show you to low mess."

I advanced rapidly in my life as a nest-maid snake for the enemy. I spent only two days in low mess providing capelin for the soldiers. Word spread that ordinary enlisted owls were eating better than the colonels and generals, and so I was soon promoted. On my third evening, just before a patrol was sent out, I began humming a tune as I served up a particularly tasty variety of capelin. It was not just any tune, but one I had found in the documents I had studied about the Great Ga'Hoole Tree.

"I say, snake." A Snowy swiveled his head toward me. "What's that ditty you're singing?"

"'The Westward Wind.'"

"'Westward Wind'? Never heard of it."

"Oh, it's a Hoolian song. It's sung at the Great Ga'Hoole Tree on the first full moon after Founder's Night."

"What are you talking about?" A Great Gray blinked at me. "How do you know all this?"

"I spent a year there, working at the great tree."

"You spent a year at the Great Ga'Hoole Tree!" The Great Gray began to bristle up. "But aren't all the snakes at the great tree blind snakes?"

"Yes, that's true," I said. "Most of them are."

"And why did you leave?"

"Well, quite frankly, they don't care for snakes that can see. I saw too much for their taste, I guess. But it was all for the best — I was homesick as well."

The Great Gray summoned a Pygmy and whispered into his ear slit.

"Yes, sir. Right away, sir."

Although I worked in the high mess, I suspected that there was one even higher. I knew that much of the fish I brought was sent elsewhere. Soon, I was being escorted out from the southernmost talon to the middle talon. The network of channels and leads through the ice there was even more complex. Deeper and deeper we went, and farther and farther from safety. The tide was coming in, which made traveling difficult and sometimes I slipped into the water to swim, with a Pygmy Owl directing me from overhead. After some time, I arrived at a ledge and was told to climb to a higher and drier one. Then, following the little Pygmy, I trailed him through a narrow passage slippery with water.

"It's an unusually high tide," the Pygmy commented to a tiny Saw-whet as we entered a cavern.

The Saw-whet looked up in alarm. "What's that snake doing here? We don't have servants here. You know that. Except for her." She tossed her head toward a snake in the corner. "She's the only other servant permitted, aside from myself. It's a security violation, you being here, especially with a stranger." She was in a twitter.

"I have an X-O Nineteen clearance," the Pygmy replied curtly. The Saw-whet blinked. I suppressed a shimmer in my scales, the natural reaction for a Kielian snake when extremely excited. I knew I was closing in.

"Is she to go into the mess?"

"Not without a blind. But he wants to talk to her," the Pygmy said.

"Hmmph!" the Saw-whet replied with more than a tinge of disapproval in her voice.

"This snake is the one who has been fishing for us."

"I wouldn't know. They only let the top officers eat the capelin." She paused. "And her, of course." The Saw-whet swiveled her head toward the snake in the corner, who cast me an anguished look. She was a cyan celadon like myself, but I had never seen a sorrier-looking snake. My scales tightened and dulled to a muddy green color. This is the closest a Kielian snake comes to wilfing. There was something very strange about this snake, even tormented, but I couldn't determine what it was.

"Go on, take a taste!" the churlish Saw-whet squawked. Terror filled the snake's eyes as she took a small peck from the midsection of the fish.

"Swallow it!" the Saw-whet commanded. "You know what happened to the last snake when they discovered she was spitting out the food. She died a worse death than any poison. Flayed, skinned alive — how would you like that?"

Then I knew. This snake was the food taster for the Monster of the Ice Massif, the Tyrant of the Talons, the Orphan Maker — Bylyric himself! No wonder this poor creature was quaking. Twice a day she was expected to test Bylyric's food. Twice a day she lived in fear of dying.

But Bylyric was here! I had found him!

"Swallow!" the Saw-whet said again. When she saw that the snake had obeyed, she began to count. When she reached one hundred, she nodded at the snake, seized the fish, and left through a small passage in the ice wall with the Pygmy following behind her. As soon as they disappeared, I turned to the snake.

"Is there another way out of here?" She looked at me with a glazed expression, then swung her head to one side indicating a small slot behind her. There were tears in her eyes, but they didn't glitter. I realized that her eyes had no luster whatsover but were a cloudy beige. A terrible dread coiled through me. I had to get out of here, but I also had to ask her, "Would you like to come with me?"

"I can't," she said softly. Then I knew why she seemed so strange, what caused the murky beige in her eyes.

"You've been excised," I said softly. She nodded. My own scales turned almost black.

To be excised was the worst thing that could happen to a Kielian snake. These hagsfiend owls had severed her extension plates, the plates that connected to the shape-shifting muscles of her head. Imagine an owl without its wings. She was the living dead.

She began to speak. "When I eat his food, I'm not afraid that I'll be poisoned. I'm afraid that I won't be. You have no idea how much I want to die. Please, please, have mercy. Kill me, I beg of you."

"Bylyric is in there, isn't he?" I said.

She nodded, then tipped her head beseechingly to one side. "Please. Kill me."

I could have finished her off swiftly. But I was so stunned I couldn't think and then I heard the sound of talons coming through the passageway. I had to get out.

"I beg you, please! You are my only chance."

What did she have to live for? Death by flaying? But it had to be quick and painless. I slammed my head down on her, and just before I struck, I saw such joy in her dull eyes. There was a tiny sparkle of green and then she was dead.

I slipped out of the cavern through the crack in the wall and slithered myself away as fast as I could. I was just about to slink out into a corridor that I thought might lead out of the middle talon when I heard the loud fluttering of the Saw-whet's wings.

"Lieutenant Jesper!" she shrieked. "The taster is dead!"

Jesper! That was Bylyric's son.

"What! Poisoned?"

"No, murdered! By that other snake that was here!"

I froze.

"Set up channel blocks immediately on every water lead. Every exit!"

I was paralyzed. With each passing second, my chances to escape were dwindling. I peeked out of the crack and slithered into the water. There was a fairly strong current, but was it going my way? I was in an ice maze, and I'd gotten badly turned around.

My first decision was to not fight the current. There was no sense in tiring myself out when I didn't know which way to swim. I took a deep dive as I didn't want to leave any trace of a wake. I surfaced for breath before I really needed to because to burst through the water gasping would be a giveaway. This worked fine until the third time I surfaced, when I heard the wing beats of several owls close by. It's said that owls are silent fliers, but that wasn't true in the tight confines of these narrow ice passages. Everything from their voices to their wing beats echoed off the ice walls and was magnified. There was a patrol coming my way. I dove quickly, still unsure which way to go.

Then I remembered how high the tide had been when the Pygmy Owl had led me to Bylyric. Now it wasn't nearly as high — the pathways I had glimpsed were no longer slippery with water. The tide must be receding, flowing back out to the sea! The current was with me. I was heading in the right direction!

In another few minutes, I could feel the turbulence of the sea pressing in upon me. I was so close! I slipped up, barely raising my eyes above the surface. The sight shocked me.

Just ahead, two dozen Great Grays and Snowies were skimming the water, fanning above the sea, searching for me. I dove as deep as I could. How long could I hold my breath? How could I ever get past this barrier of owls? A shadow passed over me, and I felt myself cringe. But it wasn't the shadow of an owl's wing. It was a strange, irregular shape that clunked up against another.

Ice! Ice bumping up against ice. Small chunks of ice that had been pulled into the channel by the incoming tide were now being sucked out again as the tide receded.

I felt a shimmer in my scales and knew exactly what to do. I must fix myself to the base of one of these ice chunks. With any luck, there might be a small crack that trapped a bubble of air beneath the water. I swam straight up to the ice chunk and sunk my fangs into the base. If there hadn't been a crack before, there was now and I wriggled my head into it until I found a pocket of air. The ice chunk sped toward the sea, faster and faster as we got to the narrow head of the channel. And then I was free.

I'm not sure how long I stayed under the ice chunk before I dared to breach the surface.

As quickly as I could, I searched out one of the snakes who had accompanied me. We sent out a code and then struck out across the ocean to our rendezvous point.

We were out, we were safe, and we had priceless information.

CHAPTER 34

Separate Paths, One Cause

The second Octavia returned, the general sent a sergeant to fetch me.

When Lil and I arrived at the general's hollow, we could tell that Octavia was exhausted.

"Octavia!" I gasped. "Are . . . are you all right?"

General Andricus stepped toward me. "She found him."

I blinked. "You found Bylyric?"

Octavia raised her head to give me a tired smile. "He's there. Middle talon of the Ice Talons."

"And you're all right?"

"Of course I'm all right! I'm just tired!" she snapped. I blessed her crankiness. It meant she was indeed okay.

The general's white face seemed to glow like a full moon in the dim light of the chamber. His voice was a hoarse whisper. "He's there and we have to move fast! We have to get him before he moves."

For years, Bylyric's precise whereabouts had been a mystery. My parents had discussed sighting him when I was just a newly hatched owlet. Just when the Kielian League thought we had him, he would seem to dissolve like mist in the sun. Some whispered that he was no mere owl, that there was something supernatural about him. But I had always known that he was just an ordinary owl with an extraordinary lust for power.

And now, thanks to Octavia's intelligence, we had him. If we could find and eliminate Bylyric, it would destroy the morale of the Ice Talons and stop their invasion in its tracks. Our plan was to get Bylyric and then surprise the Ice Talons with a full-scale invasion.

We listened carefully as Felix, a Boreal Owl who was a master cartographer, clawed at a rat-skin map of the Ice Talons. "This is the compound in the second or middle talon of the Ice Talons. Several ice notches run off the main passage. He's confined to this one. As far as we can tell, it's the only one that can accommodate his wingspan."

"Are there guards with him?"

"Of course," said Felix. Patches the snow leopard growled in agreement.

Between our best slipgizzles, Moss's matchless team of snow leopards, and a cadre of Kielian snakes, we had managed to gather excellent intelligence. Now our main fear was that Bylyric had moved again in the time since Octavia had pinpointed his location. So far, our slipgizzles in the region, including the resistance leaders, had seen no sign of this. The slipgizzles had obtained profiles on all of Bylyric's owl guards and had been able to track each one of them. The maze that constituted the Ice Talons was seemingly endless, and one could easily get lost. But the real problem was the constricted fighting space. "The big questions are," I said, "do we go in or flush him out into the open? Is it to be a full-scale air strike or a targeted raid?"

"We should plan for both," Lil said. I looked up at her.

For the first time we were to be together in battle. My gizzard clenched. I didn't know if I could stand to see Lil in such danger. When the meeting broke up, I waited in agony for the general to send word that it was time to strike.

CHAPTER 35

Operation Ice Shield

We clawed up slowly, deliberately, and in total silence. We donned our helmets — a new piece of gear Thora had designed with airfoils on the sides to increase our speed. Each owl double-checked the locking mechanisms on his or her claws. Every step in getting ready was an opportunity to focus, to ensure we were completely ready and not vulnerable to careless mistakes. Clawing up was a ritual of intense concentration. The last piece of gear we put on before taking up our weapons were our ice goggles.

We wore a new goggle design that was vastly improved. The design was a collaborative effort between Orf, Thora, and two ice harvesters, Liefa and Friedl. I had brought back samples of what I thought was an unusual kind of blue ice from the Shagdah Snurl. This ice was much bluer than the ice we'd previously used for goggles. I was impressed with its clarity and when I held it up to the sun in the brightest part of the day, I noticed that it could filter out the most blinding rays. "Imagine," I'd said, "if we could fashion protective eye covers from these.

We could do raids in the day when the enemy is blinded — we could attack in the noonday sun."[35]

We worked on the goggles for several moons and, in fact, our entire attack strategy was planned around the use of them. We were going to attack at dawn and flush Bylyric out into the blinding sun as it was rising over the horizon. It was essential that we press the advantage of the sun's glare. When the enemy came out from the protection of the ice walls of the Talons, we would force them to face east, directly into the rising sun. If they turned tail and fled west, we would lose them. We had to cut off all their exits.

For this operation, I wouldn't be flying with Octavia. She was really too large for the narrow channels of the Ice Talons and wouldn't be able to take full advantage of what we called the snakes' "swing span." So I was to carry a small but very effective snake named Albimore, a cerulean lazuli. Octavia would ride outside the Ice Shield aboard Rufus, our Spotted Owl navigator.

The silence was thick as we attached our goggles to our helmets. We would take off from Dark Fowl at night and wouldn't pull down the goggles until dawn broke.

---

35 It is widely assumed that owls cannot see well during the day. This is false. Owls can see fine during the day, but very few creatures can see well when the noonday sun is reflecting off sheets of ice.

As we lifted off, Loki looked at me, and I could tell he was thinking of those fire spikes from the Other that I had dropped into the Bitter Sea. Would they have made us feel safer than these goggles? Would the spikes have given us a deadly advantage? These were questions I wasn't prepared to answer. Besides, the fire spikes were rusting at the bottom of the sea.

As we entered the narrow ice passage that led us toward Bylyric, I felt the onslaught of new strange winds. It felt as if we were caught in a latticework of gusts. Blix was flying wing command for one of the smaller units, called chaws. She was extraordinary. We followed her path as her tiny body shuttled through the warp and weft of the gusts. The other members of the chaw steadied as we mimicked her wing motions. We might not all be Saw-whets, but we were all now flying like Blix. In the narrow channel of water below us, I saw the mottled head of a snow leopard, swimming silently. *They're with us!* I rejoiced.

It was not yet dawn, but the light in the passages was growing brighter, bouncing off the slick ice walls. In another few minutes, it would be blinding to the uncovered eyes of an owl.

We swooped around a bend, backwinging madly as we caught sight of two guards. Astonishingly, they were sound asleep! Blix silently drew one of Thora's new ice splinters and the action began. A startled guard gave a loud screech as the ice splinter pierced his shoulder. Two snow leopards sprang from the water with earsplitting screams. Enemy owls streamed out from their hollows in the ice walls.

We wheeled to begin our split maneuver. Blix looped back, skimming close to the water and underneath the enemy owls. A Pygmy Owl flew with her as a midair reloader. Blix let loose a barrage of ice splinters, pressing the Ice Talon owls east toward the rising sun.

A Whiskered Screech had swerved out of the pack and flew directly at me.

"Grip One!" I cried to Albimore. He coiled up into a spring on my back, a posture that gave him immense power. We dove beneath the Screech and came straight up under him. Between my battle claws and Albimore's fangs, we split him in two.

The other five owls in our unit, each of us with a Kielian on our back, raced ahead. The snakes swung their heads like flails, and no enemy could get near us. Albimore kept up a running report. I was dying to know if Bylyric had appeared yet. Was he one of the pursuers?

"Got a fully armed small Snowy off your starboard tail feathers," Albimore called. "Must be his son."

"Not Bylyric?" I felt my gizzard sink to my talons.

"Watch out! There's a butt-ugly Spotted Owl to port —"

Feathers streaked with blood swirled up beside me.

"Albimore! What's that?"

Albimore whooped. "Snow leopards took out a guard on the ice ridge."

We were approaching the main shaft. I could feel the suck of the wind on my wings. The air currents were immensely strong, as if we were being inhaled by some enormous creature. And then we were up and out, in the full-glare sun.

"There he is!" shrieked Albimore. And so it was! The Orphan Maker, Bylyric himself, was staggering through the blades of the rising sun. Bloodred crescents crisscrossed his facial disc, swiping over his beak and curling up beneath his eyes, which seemed to spin against the white feathers of his face. The design tilted at an odd angle and I felt myself tilting, too, as if I were hypnotized in some way. There must have been an escape hatch for Bylyric in a side notch of the ice maze. How else would he be flying here, away from the main action below?

My eyes widened and, for a second, shock locked my wings. For flying by his side — *by his side!* — was Ifghar with Gragg riding high on his back.

One thought filled my mind: *Separate them!* If I could separate Ifghar from Gragg, I could save him.

"No, Lyze! No!" Albimore cried out to me as I started to bank, but I barely heard him. I was obsessed with tearing Gragg from the back of my brother.

"What are you doing?" I screamed at Ifghar. He opened his

beak and howled maniacally, then peeled off to port. Gragg hissed and swung his head toward me.

No! Don't follow! shrieked a voice in my head. Ifghar and Gragg were baiting me, distracting me. Gragg was riding my brother's back like a succubus, a hagsfiend without wings, a witch.

I had just one thought: It was Gragg's fault! Kill Gragg and I would get my brother back. I chased them, flying very low now, just skimming the white caps of the Ice Talon straits.

"Go back! BYLYRIC!" Albimore's voice finally scratched through my anger. I looked up and saw his head tossing frantically upward.

"Oh, great Glaux!" I yelled.

Lil was advancing on Bylyric with Miss Hot Point clutched in her starboard talon. He carried a fizgig in one talon and an ice dagger in the other. Strix Struma was flying a decoy pattern to keep Bylyric heading directly into the sun, which blasted over the eastern horizon like the fire from an immense and diabolical forge. Had it not been for the goggles, our eye tubes would have been fried. *They've got him!* I thought.

Then a wind came out of nowhere, a haggish wind that threw Lil and Strix Struma into a dangerous tilt. Lil had just raised her hot lance, and the weight pulled her into a roll. She careened wildly and lost her grip on the lance, which fell into the sea.

The haggish wind kicked Bylyric over sharply so that he was no longer facing the sun. He could see again, and he screeched and advanced on Lil. He had her in his sights! Through my goggles, I could see the bright fire of lunacy burning in his eyes.

"LIL!" I shrieked.

I winged upward like a streak. I could feel Albimore rising into a strike coil on my back, the winds whizzing by his fully extended fangs.

Then the world seemed to slow. I staggered in flight as I saw Ifghar appear once more. He was closing in on Lil as well, Gragg on his back, fangs glinting. It was an ambush! Ifghar hooted something to Lil that I couldn't hear at first. Then a gust of wind snagged his cries and slammed the words into my ear slits.

"We'll die together! I love you! I've always loved you!"

I couldn't believe it. Ifghar loved Lil? Ifghar was going to kill her?

I shot up like a lava bomb from a volcano, my battle claws curved to rip my brother in two. But in my rage, I got too near to Gragg. Before I could do anything, I felt Gragg's fangs reach out and tear at my eyes. I saw blood — my own blood. Suddenly, the haggish winds were drenched in red, more blood than could possibly come from me.

From the corner of my good eye, I caught sight of Lil, her golden eyes frozen in horror.

There was an ice dagger deep in her chest, and she was spinning down and down in a slow spiral until a cresting wave below reached up and dragged her into the sea.

"NOOOO!" I screeched. It wasn't supposed to be this way! It was supposed to be Ifghar, not Lil. Not my darling Lil!

Yet through that blood I saw a clear path to Bylyric. I shot straight up to him. It was his ice dagger that had killed my Lil, and he only had one weapon now, the fizgig. He never saw me coming. I thrust my battle claws deep into him. Something dropped through the air, like a blood star out of the dawn.

"The gizzard! Bylyric's gizzard!" came the cry. To strike the gizzard is truly one chance in a million. It's so rare that it's thought to be almost magical. The battle stalled. It's as if I'd taken the gizzard of the whole Ice Talon army.

But my own gizzard was shattered as well. With my good eye, I looked down at the sea below. Lil's lovely face, eyes closed now, bobbed up once, then twice, then sank into the tumultuous water. The foam of the waves was pink with her blood.

I went kerplonken, plummeting toward my love.

THE LONG MOONS OF THE RETREAT

CHAPTER 36

End Game

This is what's so terrible about grief: You relive the final moments of your beloved's life for years and years and years. It's like flying with one wing. You never become used to it. The shock might wear off, the images grow a little dimmer. But the panic creeps back while you sleep in the brightest part of the day. My dreams are drenched now with the pink foam of the cresting waves, waves pink with the blood of my Lil. The same pink as the ice flowers she had worn on our wing-fast night, the pink of the garland she had draped over her head. I have a deep and abiding hatred of morning light now, of high noon, of anything that reminds me of the day my mate died.

I went kerplonken during the battle and when I regained consciousness, I found myself in a vacuum transport. A voice murmured to me in comforting tones, trying to reassure me. But what could anyone say? Lil was dead. I'd watched the

Everwinter Sea swallow her lacerated body. And with it, the future had died, been snuffed out — the very future of which she had spoken about so boldly to me. It was as if a knife had cut through the lovely darkness of dreams to reveal a horrible and eternal brightness that was to be my future.

We owls are creatures of the night, companions of darkness. Our dreams blossom in darkness, and in the light, they wither and die.

The voice beside me in the transport vacuum kept speaking in soothing tones. It took me a while to realize that it was Octavia. I gasped as I saw her head. It was so small, so damaged. And what was wrong with her face? Then I realized it was her eyes — they were gone. I gasped.

"Octavia, what happened to you?"

"They got my eyes with a billy hook." She chuckled, but it wasn't her usual raucous laughter. "I can be a nest-maid snake now, like the ones in the Southern Kingdoms."

"No! No!" I couldn't believe it. My dear Octavia had been trying to comfort me when she had lost both her eyes.

The boisterous winds rocked us as the owls carried us toward the Glauxian Brothers retreat on the Bitter Sea.

The Glauxian Brothers were renowned for their healing arts, but they couldn't restore Octavia's eyes. My own eye injury was minor in comparison. I have fierce scars around the socket and I can't see out of it as well as before. But it was my talon that bothered me more. An Eagle Owl had grabbed me as I fell toward the sea and had broken one of my talons. The brothers tried their best to set it and gave me ointments and salves to rub into it. But the pain was almost constant and finally one night I'd had enough and I bit it off. What did I need a talon for? I was never going to hold a weapon again. I hung up my battle claws and swore never to put them on. I could hunt perfectly well with my remaining talons.

Octavia and I shared a hollow in one of a large circle of birch trees that composed the Glauxian Brothers retreat. The brothers were bound by a vow of silence, but they weren't quite as strict about it as the Glauxian Sisters. They spent a good deal of the night chanting. There were several Boreal Owls among them, whose voices rang like chimes against the silver of the birches.

I sank into a deep depression. For months on end, I hardly left the hollow except to hunt. It's difficult for me to explain the strange feelings that afflicted me. I could not speak about them to anyone, not even to Octavia. Lil's death was a wound that never healed. I thought at first that if I committed my feelings to verse and wrote about her, it would help.

But each time I completed a poem, it was like peeling off a fresh scab.

This was one I wrote after an evening hunt:

> There is a gutter in the wind
> Where once she flew.
> A hole in the night,
> A bit from the moon.
> A blankness
> A void
> That absence
> That Lil!
> This nothingness consumes me
> The long shadow of a love vanished
> In a world that burns too bright.

Octavia tended to my needs meticulously. She was becoming a nest-maid snake after all. It saddened me in many ways. She was so bright that it seemed a waste of time to me that she should spend her days slurping up vermin and keeping my hollow tidy. She even started to run her fangs lightly through my feathers to comb out my burrs. When I complained that she was squandering her talents, she very nicely told me to shut up. She said that what she did with her time was her business, and she didn't relish living with a slob.

Little did I know that Octavia was hatching her own schemes. I don't use the term "hatching" lightly here, for her schemes were aimed at bringing me new life.

To say Octavia was fed up with my ways is perhaps an understatement. But she was also worried — worried sick, she told me later. She said it was as if I were withering away. She knew I had chronic pain in my injured talon, but after I bit it off and the pain vanished, she saw no improvement in me.

Octavia can be chary with her words. In fact, unlike most creatures, I learned over the years that the less Octavia says, the more intensely she's thinking. So one day she went to Brother Oliver's study hollow, just off the Glauxian retreat library. I know of this only because Brother Oliver died recently, and a peregrine messenger delivered me his diary. I've copied his words exactly:

An extraordinary thing happened tonight, shortly after evensong. The words of the Glaux canticle were still ringing in my ear slits when the snake Octavia arrived. She is of a turquoise hue, a cyan celadon to be exact and, poor thing, she's blind — she lost her eyes in the terrible Battle of the Ice Talons. She came to the retreat two moons before with the renowned Whiskered Screech Lyze, the Major General of the Glauxspeed Division. He refuses to answer to his military title now; indeed, he has completely renounced his rank and vowed never to fight again. Lyze and Octavia were both wounded, although Lyze's injury appears to be one of the mind more than the body. That's what Octavia came to speak with me about.

"I can see you are troubled," I said, hoping to offer a sympathetic ear slit.

"Indeed, Brother Oliver."

"It's Lyze, I suspect."

"You suspect right." She inhaled sharply. "Lyze bit off his own talon because it was causing him so much pain. But now . . . but now . . ."

"But now," I interjected, "the pain is gone, but the misery persists — like a scroom of what was."

"Exactly!" she exclaimed. She paused as if trying to organize her thoughts. "Poor Lyze is pursued by many scrooms — most of all by the memory of his beloved mate, Lil. But there's one thing that's still alive for him, although I fear it will die soon if he doesn't use it."

I must admit, I was a bit perplexed.

"Go on," I urged.

"He hasn't engaged his mind. If he doesn't soon, I'm afraid he'll lose it!"

I felt my gizzard tighten. Everyone knew that this Whiskered Screech, hatched on Stormfast Island, was one of the most brilliant owls in the Northern Kingdoms. He knew weather. He knew winds. His mind was fantastically perceptive and analytical. Now it was my turn to stammer.

"It — it has surprised me that he has not taken more interest in our library."

"Yes — for a mind like that to not have once peeked into this hollow with its rich collection of manuscripts and parchments! It's surprising and disturbing."

"And what might we do about that?" I asked Octavia. Her answer stunned me.

"I want to be his eyes!"

"B-b-b-but, how can you?" I stammered again.

"You must read to me — anything from this library. It doesn't matter what, but anything about the winds of the Shagdah Snurl would be particularly good. About the winds, not the legends, but physical descriptions, observations. He'll like that. And I'll —"

"You'll tell him about it? You'll memorize it?"

"Not exactly," she said. "I plan to write it down."

"Can you write?" I didn't mean it as an insult, but many Kielian snakes couldn't!

"Of course I can write!" she snapped. "What do you take me for, a nincompoop?" Then she seemed to shrink up and falter. "I mean, I used to be able to write. And I have been practicing."

"How can you practice if you can't see?"

"I can feel!" She had brought a small piece of parchment with her and she unfurled it. "Touch it!" she ordered. "With your third talon port side."

This is an owl's most sensitive talon. I did as she told me.

"I feel bumps," I said. I was utterly confused.

"Yes! But there is a pattern to the bumps. I punctured it with my own fangs, just as I used to dip them in ink pots to write."

"What does it say?" I asked.

"It says my name is Octavia. I was born on Stormfast Island. I was a big, fat creature and lazy as could be until I met Lyze — Lyze of Kiel, creator of the Glauxspeed Division, who saved my life and made me into a decent creature. That's what it says."

I thought that I saw tears glistening in the dents that had been her eyes. "And if I can read to Lyze, perhaps I can rescue him, just as he rescued me."

I had never seen a snake more determined.

CHAPTER 37

A Reprise

That, dear readers, is exactly what happened. Blind Octavia led me back to books, to science, to research, and rekindled the dwindling flames of my mind. My steadfast friend Octavia stirred the coals that were quickly becoming cinders — the cinders that would have led to complete dementia. Soon, she was much more than a nest-maid snake. She was my research assistant and, with her odd bumpy writing, my note taker. The sound of her fangs puncturing parchment was a new kind of music, one that seemed to blend with the lovely hymns of evensong and the wind shivering through the trees.

Some creatures have a destiny thrust upon them that is at odds with their true nature. War and leadership had been thrust on me by my parents, by the times, and by the spreading bile of Bylyric's evil. Left to my own, I wanted nothing to do with war. I only wanted to explore the mysteries of our Earth and its creatures. Science was my great love, but the ferschtucken War of the Ice Talons kept getting in the way.

It was at the Glauxian Brothers retreat — a place where faith was as much a part of life as air — that I made some of my most significant scientific discoveries. I observed, tested, and proved certain notions that I had speculated on for years.

When the war died down, I went to the hatching place of the winds again and again, always accompanied by Octavia. Some of my ideas I had to discard, but others I managed to prove.

I have no problem with the stories or legends my fellow owls seemed to love. I had no problem with the Glauxian Brothers' deep faith. Faith is a personal thing after all. None of the Brothers would force their faith upon me. They simply choose to picture the world in a different way. As Brother Oliver said to me once, "There's room for both, you know. There's more than one way to tell a story."

The War of the Ice Claws did eventually come to an end, but none too soon. Bylyric's son, Jesper, rose to prominence, inheriting the raging remnants of his father's force. But a Glauxspeed assassination unit led by Strix Struma, Loki, and Blix cornered him in a remote region of the H'rathghar. And it was Patches, the snow leopard I'd injured, who actually delivered the fatal blow to him with one of her immense paws.[36]

---

36 One might also consider the weapon of Patch's paw to be somewhat ironic. For the paws of a snow leopard, though immense and powerful, are lined with fur for better traction on the ice. Thus, it has been said that snow leopards can deliver the "soft blow that kills."

I never learned what happened to Ifghar. Never asked and no one ever told me. It was better that way. I had to put him out of my mind and out of my life, or bitterness would consume me.

Long before the end of the war, news came to me that Thora had decamped and flown to the Southern Kingdoms. She wanted to create art, not weapons. Like me, she was done with war.

Every now and then, Loki or Blix or Moss would show up at the retreat and try to entice me to return to Dark Fowl as an instructor. But I had no interest. I was completely occupied with my research, and the Glauxian Brothers library was a Glauxsend for me.

One day, I heard a whispering outside my hollow.

"I'll see," I heard Octavia say from just outside the hollow. "But don't count on it."

"Don't count on what, Octavia?"

"You have a visitor, Lyze."

"Blix and Rufus were here just last moon. I told them then and I'll tell them again, I have no interest in becoming an instructor."

A familiar voice broke in. "They're called rybs at the Great Ga'Hoole Tree, Lyze. Rybs, not instructors."

I nearly dropped my plummels. "Thora!" I exclaimed.

"None other."

"B-b-but I thought you were in the Southern Kingdoms!"

"Indeed. I have a forge in Silverveil. I make beautiful things, Lyze — sculpture from metal. I haven't made a weapon in — let's see, nigh on five years."

She planted herself before me and glared. "Now listen to me, you stubborn old Whiskered Screech. You've grieved too long. Grief becomes an indulgence after a certain point."

I looked at her narrowly. "What are you trying to say?"

"Come with me! Come back to the Great Ga'hoole Tree. Come be a teacher, a ryb."

"I don't want to teach about war."

"You don't have to. In the Hoolian dialect, 'ryb' means 'learned one.' You've been exploring, researching all these years. Why not share it? There is a library at the great tree that makes this one look pathetic."

"Don't tell Brother Oliver that," Octavia said.

Thora swiveled her head around. "He knows it. Who do you think sent a peregrine to tell me what Lyze has been up to? Octavia can come with you and continue to be your assistant."

I shook my head wearily. "But it's impossible, Thora. Don't you understand — they'll know me. Everyone knows about Major General Lyze of Kiel, creator of the Glauxspeed Division. The division that won the War of the Ice Claws."

"No!" said another voice. Brother Oliver crammed into the hollow.

"You won't be known as Major General Lyze of Kiel."

"Well, what in the name of Glaux would I be known as?"

"Ezylryb," Brother Oliver said softly. "Ezylryb! And you will become the greatest ryb the Great Ga'Hoole Tree has ever seen."

I swung my head toward Octavia. Although she couldn't see me, she had developed extraordinary sensibilities and seemed to know when I was looking at her and what I might say before I said it. But for this no words were really needed. She nodded ever so slightly, and I could see what she was thinking:

Do it!

Epilogue

And so I have been a ryb at this grand old tree for decades. Now a young Barn Owl has arrived with his three friends. I can tell he will make a great leader, possibly even become a king of this great tree. You blink? Of course you do, for it's a preposterous notion. To become king of the great tree, one must be born to royalty or "embered" as decreed by the prophecy of Hoole. Ridiculous, you say. But I say destiny has nothing to do with it. Only inner nobility and intelligence are what count in the end.

So, dear reader, would you care to make a wager on my friend Soren? For I see genius where others might not.

Author's Note

As so often happens, I have been inspired by other artists, and I wish to acknowledge and give credit where credit is due. In Chapter 8 when Tantya Hanja bursts into song at the grog tree, the song she sings was completely inspired by Bob Dylan's "The Times They Are A-Changin'," a ballad written at the height of the Vietnam War whose lyrics went beyond the war to address social and racial issues. The names for the different kinds of snow were taken — although not exactly — from an Inuit lexicon that describes more kinds of snow than I could have ever imagined. The myschgrad serpent that the blink skog of Dark Fowl tells a story about is based on the legendary Midgard serpent of the Norse sagas.